"I don't know what you think you are doing."

As her head disappeared into the folds of the dress she wondered why she should harbor the utterly wanton wish that his hands had followed the quite blatant track of his eyes.

"I am trying to hurry proceedings along," he answered, forcing a lazy tone to disguise his sudden feeling of breathlessness. That had been his true intention, but it had been a mistake.

She had a truly beautiful body—lush, ripe and tempting. Looking at the bountiful curves that almost seemed to be pleading to be freed of the unnatural constraint of confining white cotton was not enough. He wanted to touch.

We're delighted to announce that

A Mediterranean Marriage

is taking place in
Harlequin Presents

This month, in *The Italian's Wife*
by Diana Hamilton

you are invited to the wedding of
Lucenzo Verdi and Portia Makepeace

Portia has fallen in love with Lucenzo Verdi, and
has agreed to marry him—but knows he believes
her to be a gold digger. Has she managed to
convince her passionate Italian of her innocence
or does his marriage proposal hide other plans?

More in our exciting miniseries
A MEDITERRANEAN MARRIAGE
coming soon!

Diana Hamilton

THE ITALIAN'S BRIDE

A Mediterranean Marriage

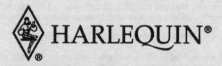

HARLEQUIN®

TORONTO • NEW YORK • LONDON
AMSTERDAM • PARIS • SYDNEY • HAMBURG
STOCKHOLM • ATHENS • TOKYO • MILAN • MADRID
PRAGUE • WARSAW • BUDAPEST • AUCKLAND

ISBN 0-373-12262-4

THE ITALIAN'S BRIDE

First North American Publication 2002.

Copyright © 2001 by Diana Hamilton.

Visit us at www.eHarlequin.com

Printed in U.S.A.

CHAPTER ONE

'I'LL get it,' Portia offered much too brightly as the strident ring of the doorbell broke the tense silence.

Visitors to the small semi on the outskirts of the industrial Midlands town of Chevington, where she had lived with her parents for the whole of her twenty-one years, were rare—and certainly not expected at nine o'clock on a damp April evening.

She was out of the neatly furnished sitting room before her father could get to his feet and tell her to stay where she was. The idea of leaving baby Sam with her mother did not even enter her head. Dealing with the caller, even if it turned out to be just someone asking for directions, would be a welcome distraction from her parents' tight-lipped unspoken disapproval.

Enfolding her tiny baby more securely in his shawl, Portia tucked a wandering strand of pale blonde hair behind her ear and opened the front door just as an impatient finger jabbed again at the bell-push. Her always-ready smile was wiped away when she saw who it was.

One of the frighteningly powerful, disgustingly wealthy Verdi clan. It just had to be!

How many times had she told herself that they would never know what had happened, and that even if they did—through some cruel quirk of fate—not a single one of them would be interested in either her or her illegitimate child.

It looked as if she couldn't have been more wrong, she thought sickly as her stomach nose-dived down to the soles of her feet and shot right back again.

Everything about this stranger betrayed his Italian heritage, from the proud tilt of that arrogantly held dark head, the black eyes that regarded her so narrowly from beneath slashing brows, the high-bridged aquiline nose, to the shockingly sensual mouth. The family connection was painfully obvious, she conceded as her stomach tied itself in knots again.

He wasn't as playboy-pretty as Vito had been; the cynical lines that bracketed his mouth, the harsher cast of his features saw to that. And he was a good head taller and at least half a dozen years older than Vito had been.

Vito, the father of her baby, had been twenty-six years old when he'd died, six weeks and four days ago...

Vito had deceived both her and his wife, and probably dozens of other gullible females as well...

Jumbled thoughts raced around inside her head—the head that her parents had always disappointedly maintained to be empty of anything more solid than fluff—and the stranger intoned, 'Portia Makepeace?'

She couldn't speak. Her vocal cords, usually so active, had gone into shock. She'd been found and she hadn't wanted to be. Who knew what the powerfully influential Verdi clan would do? Try to take Vito's son from her because he was one of their own? It didn't bear thinking about!

Too late she attempted what she should have done earlier—to shut the door in his face—but he shouldered his way into the cramped hall. His narrowed eyes tracked a disparaging path over her tumbled shoulder-length hair, the old blue dressing gown belted tightly around her far too generous curves, the ridiculous slippers that looked like frogs—a going-to-maternity-hospital gift from her friend Betty—and back up to lock with huge grey eyes that were annoyingly swimming with tears, before sliding down to stare intently at two-week-old Sam, held protectively in her arms.

'Too ashamed to speak? That I can understand, although I admit it's unexpected,' he said grimly, his voice deep, only slightly accented. 'But I don't suppose you're going to try to pretend you are not what you are—a husband-stealer—or that I am not uncle to your child. That wouldn't suit your purposes, would it? You'll be happy to know that I recognise you from the day of Vittorio's funeral.'

Her head spinning giddily, Portia gulped. Happy? Of course she wasn't! Having one of them track her down was the last thing she'd wanted.

But she might have known. Hadn't her parents warned her that attending her dead lover's funeral, running the gauntlet of his prestigious family, not to mention his grieving widow, would be a mistake of the most tasteless kind?

But she'd gone anyway; she'd felt as if she simply

had to—intending only to slip in quietly, hide at the back of the congregation where she would be unnoticed. The softness of her heart had overridden the shock of her recent discovery: the knowledge that Vito had never loved her and had run the proverbial mile when she'd told him she was expecting their child. She'd needed to pay her last respects to the father of her unborn baby, to say one last goodbye, to pray for him.

Eight months pregnant, and huge with it, hiding hadn't been easy, and remaining unnoticed had become out of the question when, overcome with mixed but strong emotions, she had fainted.

She had only vague memories of being helped outside. Someone had fetched a glass of water. A female and two males, talking in rapid Italian above her spinning head, dark suspicious eyes inspecting her closely, had made her want to sink right back into oblivion. But when she'd recovered enough to reluctantly mumble her home address, when pressed, one of the men had used his mobile to summon a taxi. Into which she'd been thankfully and discreetly bundled—something rather suspect to be removed from the scene as quickly as possible.

She had thought—devoutly hoped—that that was the end of it. But plainly it hadn't been. Unconsciously running a feather-light finger over her sleeping baby's velvet-soft cheek, she at last found her tongue and uttered staunchly, 'I've nothing to be ashamed of. Nothing!'

She'd loved Vito, admired him when he'd told her

he was working hard, saving to open his own restaurant, had believed him when he'd told her he loved her, too, and that they'd marry as soon as it was financially possible.

She hadn't known he was already married, that everything he'd said to her was untrue. He had promised marriage and happy-ever-after because he must have thought it was the only way to get her to agree to spending that weekend with him.

So what right had this hard-faced man to look at her as if she were something utterly despicable? Her voice thickening, she demanded, 'Why are you here?'

'Good question,' he responded drily, noting the way she deliberately drew attention to the newest member of the Verdi family. He pushed his fists into the pockets of the exquisitely tailored mohair coat he was wearing, his impressive shoulders stiffening. 'Not by my own wish, you understand. To set the record straight, I was dead against the family having any contact whatsoever with you.'

His mouth thinned as he explained, 'A crumpled letter from a Portia Makepeace was found on the floor of the wreck of Vittorio's car. It gave this address.' His face darkened with distaste. 'It was hysterical. I thought it had been written by a schoolgirl, not a full-grown educated woman. Then I recalled the unknown pregnant female at the funeral, the attention she'd drawn to herself, the home address she had given. After that it didn't require the services of an Einstein to arrive at the facts. The child is my half-brother's.'

The thought of denying it didn't enter her head, but

his disparaging words had lit a rare spark of rage in her brain.

She hadn't been hysterical when she'd written to Vito at the classy London restaurant where he'd worked as a pastry chef—remembering his instructions never to phone him there because it would get him in deep trouble with his boss—she'd simply been worried half out of her mind.

She hadn't heard from him for weeks, not since she'd told him the last time he'd phoned her of her pregnancy. She'd been sure something dreadful had happened to him. It had been the only thing she'd been able to think of to explain his failure to keep in touch with her.

Now she knew why he'd washed his hands of her, knew that everything he'd ever said to her had been lies, and in her own essentially practical way she was learning to accept it. But this stranger's unforgivable scathing comment about her lack of ability when it came to the written word touched a nerve that had been raw since her early childhood.

Grey eyes glinting, she bit out sarcastically, 'I'm sorry I'm not a reincarnation of William Shakespeare.' She clamped her teeth together to stop them chattering. She was shaking all over. Whether from rage or the chilliness of the narrow hallway she didn't know, but she strongly suspected the former. 'I'd like you to leave,' she ordered tightly.

She should have saved her breath, she thought irately. The patronising brute simply stood his ground, one ebony brow lifting derisively, a smile that held not even a flicker of warmth lifting one corner of that long, sensual mouth. 'Pushing your luck, aren't you? I might just take you at your word and report my mission as a failure.' The ersatz smile disappeared at the speed of light, and his features were hard-edged as he added softly, 'I'm quite sure that is not what you have in mind.'

He'd bet his last million lire it wasn't! Despite the impression given by that deranged-sounding letter—bleating on about wedding plans and the baby they were expecting—this woman was no dumb klutz.

She would have continued to bombard the holding address—the astronomically expensive restaurant Vittorio had habitually frequented—with those whining, schoolgirlish letters no doubt changing in tone after the birth to demands for high levels of maintenance—or else!

But Vittorio had been tragically killed behind the wheel of one of the fast cars he'd been addicted to. So her modus operandi had changed.

Watching her intently, he expelled a sigh between his gritted teeth. He might have been inclined to give her the benefit of the doubt had she not muscled in on the private family funeral with that fainting fit which, with hindsight, he decided had to have been manufactured to make double sure of being noticed.

As if that large lumpen thing, covered in a shabby brown coat and making snuffling noises into a huge handkerchief, could have been overlooked by any one of the elegantly black-attired members of the family!

It had been the action of a woman who was out to

make trouble. He sighed, not liking what he was having to do. But his father, once the contents of that letter had been made known, had been adamant.

He dragged air deep into his lungs. It stuck in his craw, but he was going to have to extend the invitation.

'Portia—what are you doing? Who is it?' At that moment Godfrey Makepeace emerged from the sitting room, his voice tight with the strain he'd been under since learning of his daughter's pregnancy and the simultaneous disappearance of the man responsible— the man he'd taken an instant dislike to on the one and only occasion they'd met.

'It's OK, Dad.' She turned to him, her heart contracting guiltily. He looked so careworn, with his fawn cardigan buttoned so neatly across his narrow chest, his bald head gleaming in the overhead light. Once again she'd failed him—and her mother—this time monumentally.

Portia felt really dreadful about it. They'd both impressed on her all the logical reasons why she should have had an abortion, and when logic had failed they'd resorted to pleading. But she had adamantly refused to destroy the new little life growing inside her. It wasn't the poor mite's fault that his father had been a lying deceiver.

'This gentleman,' she stressed coldly, 'is just leaving.'

But the 'gentleman' had ideas of his own. Portia pulled an angry face as he stepped forward with all the spine-tingling predatory grace of a great jungle cat, his hand outstretched.

'Mr Makepeace—Lucenzo Verdi. Vittorio was my half-brother. I apologise for intruding at this hour, but I've only just returned from Florence with an urgent communication from my father, Eduardo Verdi, the head of our family.' He paused for a moment to let the information sink in and Portia could have slapped him.

Because of the press coverage following Vito's fatal accident everyone knew of the awe-inspiring international success of the Verdi Mercantile Bank and the position Vito had held in its London headquarters. Trust this creep to rub their humble noses in his family's power and wealth!

One of Sam's hands escaped from the shawl and his tiny body stiffened in her loving arms. Portia barely registered her father's guarded 'And?' as she gazed, entranced, at the shock of dark soft hair, the unfocused milky blue eyes that she was sure would one day turn to grey, just like her own.

Her baby was ready for his next feed and that, for the moment, was her overriding priority. Let whatsisname—Lucenzo—make his 'communication' and sling his hook. Her father would relay the details and she would ignore them.

And if there was a threat—implied or openly stated—that the family would fight for custody of her son, then she and Sam would simply disappear.

On that heartening but slightly scary determination she inched past the overbearing presence of the Italian, and the much smaller frame of her father, and headed for the kitchen to warm up the bottle of formula she'd stored in the fridge.

Forty-five minutes later she reluctantly laid a sleepy, contented Sam in the crib at the side of her single bed and went downstairs, her ridiculous slippers sliding on the shiny linoleum that covered the narrow treads.

The Italian would have left by now. Such humble surroundings wouldn't be to his exalted taste. She would ask her parents what his famous communication had been about. Not that she was interested, but to ignore the Visitation from On High would rub her parents up the wrong way. And that, she admitted on a draining sigh, was something she'd been doing for most of her life.

Hooking her long, unkempt hair behind her ears, she took a deep, fortifying breath and walked into the sitting room. Her face drained of colour when she noted the impressively lean and moody frame reclining in the place of honour—her father's armchair at the side of the electric fire—his elegantly long legs and obviously disgustingly expensive shoes stretched out on the hearthrug.

The way the arrogantly held dark head turned to her, those black eyes glittering beneath slightly lowered lids studying her as if she were a hitherto undiscovered and not very pleasant form of insect life, made her heart contract violently beneath her breastbone and then perform a series of lazy somersaults.

'Portia—' Her mother's voice, far softer, lighter than usual, gave her the impetus to drag her part-fascinated, part-horrified gaze from that wickedly handsome, chillingly intimidating face. She gulped in a lungful of air and felt something prickly dance up and down her spine.

Joyce Makepeace was patting the empty space beside her on the sofa in invitation. Portia's soft mouth fell open. Her mother's cheeks were a becoming pink, her hazel eyes bright, her mouth smiling. The stern retired schoolmistress was actually looking fluttery!

Obeying the summons because she couldn't think of anything else to do, Portia blundered forwards, tripping over her cumbersome slippers, feeling hot and bothered, ridiculous. She wished she'd never set eyes on the things. She was only wearing them because Betty had bought them for her. That had been really sweet of her, and her conscience would have pricked unbearably if she'd put them in the bin as her father had suggested.

Making it to the sofa without further mishap, she glanced nervously at her mother, expecting the usual frown of pained displeasure for her clumsiness. Instead she received an amazing smile, a fond pat of her hand—just as if she'd done something her parents could be proud of for once, instead of falling over her feet, making a spectacle of herself.

'Signor Verdi—Lucenzo—' Joyce Makepeace dimpled '—has something to say to you, Portia.'

A fleeting smile for Joyce curled his satanically beautiful mouth as he got lithely to his feet. His piercingly dark eyes fastened on Portia's nervous face as he reached for the elegantly tailored charcoal overcoat he'd discarded and draped the soft folds over his arm.

If it weren't for the facts he wouldn't believe it. The charming, feckless, utterly faithless Vito had had many affairs—a gene he had inherited from the English girl his father had married five years after his first wife, Lucenzo's mother, had died. A year later Christine had given birth to Vittorio and, her duty done, as she'd seen it, she'd embarked on a string of unsavoury affairs.

Lucenzo tightened his mouth with grim distaste. His half-brother had favoured svelte, stylish, long-legged blondes. So what had he been doing with this overweight, clumsy creature? A blonde, admittedly, but there any point of reference ceased. Her hair was a mess and no self-respecting female would stick her feet into bright green things that looked like giant bloated frogs!

She must have caught Vittorio in an off-moment, possibly when he'd been drunk, and thrown herself at him...

'You must excuse me. I'm already late for an appointment.' Lucenzo made a point of glancing at the thin gold watch on his flat wrist. He'd had as much as he could take. Despite his warnings to his father, Portia Makepeace was about to receive all her avaricious, scheming little heart had dreamed of. The knowledge made him want to punch holes in the wall.

He eyed her coldly. 'Your parents will relay my father's wishes.' He gave her a bleak, informal nod of the head. It was more than he'd thought he could manage. 'I will see you in six weeks' time. One of my secretaries will contact you regarding the exact time and date.'

'One' of his secretaries? How many did the man have? And just what did he mean about seeing her again in six weeks' time? That was all Portia could think about as her father, looking really sprightly for a change, showed the Italian out.

And her mother said knowingly, 'If you ever want to know the meaning of the word "exotic" just think about Lucenzo Verdi! And such a gentleman, too. Quite unlike that half-brother of his. I knew he was a rogue the moment I set eyes on him.'

'You only met him once,' Portia reminded her glumly.

She'd practically had to drag Vito here. But they'd been talking about getting engaged and she'd insisted he must meet her parents. And he'd been begging her to spend a weekend with him.

'Somewhere quiet and off the beaten track,' he'd said. 'It needn't be expensive, and if you're adamant about not wasting money on an engagement ring a weekend together would be a wonderful way of marking the occasion, making it special—you know how much I love and want you, *carissima*—or do you like torturing me?'

'Once was quite enough. Anyone with a grain of intelligence would have seen through him,' Joyce remarked drily, and Portia felt the too-ready tears sting the backs of her eyes.

Did everyone else on the planet have more nous

than she did? Were her parents right when they accused her of being everyone's best friend, of being too naive to see harm in any living soul, reckless enough to fill the outstretched palms of every beggar she came across?

Not really, she defended herself. She'd seen harm in Lucenzo Verdi the moment she'd opened the door to him, hadn't she? And if her mother had heard the things he'd said to her then 'gentleman' was the last thing she would have called him!

Clutching at straws, she asked hopefully, 'Did you explain I didn't know Vito was married? That I had no idea his family was rolling in money?'

She hadn't been given the chance to explain all that herself, and even if she had been she had the gut feeling he wouldn't have believed her. But coming from her parents, who were so obviously completely respectable...

'It wasn't necessary. Once we'd established that his brother was the man you'd been seeing—the man who'd got you pregnant—there seemed no point in speaking ill of the dead. A loss like that must be difficult to bear. It hardly seemed appropriate to rub Lucenzo's nose in his brother's shortcomings.'

And no point in defending their daughter's integrity, Portia thought miserably, twisting the fabric of her shabby dressing gown between her fingers. She remembered seeing Vito's face on the front page of their daily paper. It had been a shock she hadn't really come to terms with yet. It still made her feel physically sick when she thought about the accompanying text.

Vittorio Verdi, younger son of Eduardo Verdi, international banker, was tragically killed when his Ferrari left the road. His passenger, model Kristi Hall, survived the accident and is said to be in a stable condition. Vittorio leaves a grieving widow…

Trying to swallow the huge lump in her throat, Portia scrambled to her feet, muttering thickly, 'I'm going to bed.'

'Don't you want to hear what your child's grand-father is proposing?'

Her mother sounded appalled. Portia blinked at her and sniffed miserably. 'Dad?'

'Try not to be so stupid! His Italian grandfather, of course!'

'Oh.' She'd had that particular epithet flung at her too often to even notice it now, and wrinkled her brow as she wondered how to explain her deep desire to bury her head in the sand and not know. She would rather save the nitty-gritty until the morning, when she would be better able to cope with husband-stealing recriminations or, far worse, threats to take her to court to gain custody of her precious baby son. What chance would she stand against the wealth and clout of the powerful Verdi clan?

Aware that her mother was bristling with impatience at her inability to come up with any response more intelligent than 'oh', Portia was deeply thankful to be saved from having to do anything more than just stand there when her father entered the room.

He was rubbing his hands, smiling widely. 'That is

one fine young man. Classy, but no side on him.' He beamed at his daughter, her eyes huge in the pallor of her face, 'So how does it feel to be six weeks away from going to live in pampered luxury in sunny Tuscany?'

CHAPTER TWO

'I COULD still change my mind,' Portia said, her voice shaking with a sudden, positively ferocious flood of nerves. She swallowed hard, then took a deep breath to steady herself. 'Even now,' she emphasised hopefully.

Even when Lucenzo Verdi was expected at any moment—when her luggage was filling the narrow hall and Sam was peacefully asleep in his carry cot at her feet, fed, changed and ready to go.

'Don't be so ridiculous!' The note of sheer horror in Joyce Makepeace's voice turned to grinding exasperation as she swung round from peering through the net curtains and told her daughter, 'We've been through this a thousand times over the last six weeks! Of course you can't change your mind. You have to go. What else is there?'

She expelled an impatient breath and came out with the usual well-worn litany. 'If you'd concentrated at school instead of living in a dream world you might have been equipped for a decent career, been able to afford a place of your own, proper childcare. Your father and I can't afford to keep you and the baby—'

'I could go back to work—'

'Your job's gone.'

'I could get another. In any case, Mr Weston said

he'd take me back. The girl he hired when I took maternity leave knows she's only temporary.'

'And expect me to babysit, I suppose? And keep yourself and a child on a waitress's wages? I don't think so.' Joyce's mouth thinned. 'He won't stay a baby for ever.'

Portia bit down hard on her wobbling lower lip. It was true. The job she'd enjoyed, even though humble, had paid very little. Tips were what waitresses relied on, Mr Weston had explained. The only trouble was, the type of people who frequented Joe's Place couldn't afford tips. They were mostly senior citizens lingering over a single cup of tea and a bun while they chatted to their friends as an after-shopping treat.

And apart from the dearth of tips she'd often bought hearty cheese or ham sandwiches with her own money for one particular elderly lady who'd come in on pension day and always sat on her own, never ordering more than a cup of tea. She'd looked so frail and white, as if a puff of wind would blow her over, and so pathetically grateful when Portia had slid the plate in front of her, making up some excuse or other for why the food was surplus to requirements, so that the old dear wouldn't feel she was receiving charity.

No. Her eyes misted with tears as she gazed down at her sleeping son. The only thing she could give him was love, by the bucketful.

'Sam's Italian grandfather is a very wealthy man. He can give you and the baby everything you could want,' her father said, his tone gentler than her mother's had been. 'And in that letter from him—the one his son left for you—he did say that if you weren't happy in Italy you could return to England.'

At her mother's tart 'Heaven forbid!' Portia swallowed the huge lump in her throat and tried to get rid of the scary feeling that had been steadily growing inside her all morning.

The letter, when she'd forced herself to read it, hadn't been full of recriminations or threats to take her baby from her, she reminded herself unsteadily. Eduardo Verdi had sounded like a really nice old gentleman, expressing the wish to see not only his grandson but her, too, to welcome them both into his family. He had invited them to stay for as long as they liked, the longer the better.

So what was there to be frightened of? Why the angst? She might not have the brain of a rocket scientist, but she was determined enough, strong enough, to make sure that she did what was best for her baby. And if things didn't work out in Tuscany—if, say, she found the Italian side of her son's family taking him over, sidelining her and depriving him of the most important thing for his welfare, his mother's love and devotion—then she'd pack their bags and they'd make tracks.

Alongside their passports in her handbag she had the remains of her savings—enough, surely, to pay their air fare back, she comforted herself.

'He's here.' Joyce dropped the corner of the net curtain and walked briskly out into the hall. 'Get a move on, Portia. We don't want to keep him waiting.'

Her eyes welling with tears, Portia slung her bag

over her shoulder and lifted the carry cot. They couldn't wait to be rid of her and Sam. Not that she could blame them. She had always been a huge disappointment to her parents and presenting them with an illegitimate grandchild had been the last straw.

Lucenzo Verdi was scowling at the untidy pile of her luggage, looking mean and moody in an exquisitely cut pale grey suit, a darker grey silk shirt and deep blue tie. Dark eyes glittered at her beneath broodingly lowered lids, making her feel clumsy and inept as she slowly negotiated the cot around the angle of the doorframe.

'What is this?' Lucenzo glared at the tottering pile of bulging plastic carriers and cardboard boxes that rested on top of her shabby suitcase as if they were emitting some very nasty smells.

Portia, resisting the impulse to slap that handsome oh-so-superior face, gritted her teeth and relayed defensively, 'Sam's things, mostly. Babies don't travel light.'

At the same time her mother hissed out of the corner of her tight, bright smile, 'Didn't I tell you there was no need to take so much.'

'Everything the child needs is at the Villa Fontebella,' Lucenzo stated flatly. 'All that is needed is a change of clothing for the journey.'

Not that he knew anything of children's needs, he thought heavily. His own child had died before it could be born. But it was bad enough to have to escort one of Vittorio's cast-off bimbos back to Tuscany without being lumbered with a heap of clutter that resembled a pile of rubbish left out for the refuse collectors.

Portia lifted her chin, her large grey eyes narrowing. Start as you mean to go on. Be assertive and brave for once in your life, she told herself as she took a deep breath and said shakily, 'Sam needs his own things. Neither of us is going anywhere without them.'

Her stockpile of tins of baby formula, feeding bottles, steriliser, nappies, Babygros, creams and lotions, his special shampoo, not to mention all those cute fluffy toys which were valued gifts from friends and neighbours—she wasn't prepared to leave a single thing behind.

They were all links with the safe and the known, and if she was going to have to live amongst strangers she was going to need them to cling onto, like a mental safety rope.

'I'll give you a hand.' As if sensing insurrection, Godfrey Makepeace grabbed several carriers and headed for the door.

Portia felt her mother's hand grip her arm, urging her forward as she muttered impatiently, 'Don't be tiresome! Look, I know you're nervous about going to stay with strangers, but there's no need. When your father phoned Signor Verdi senior to make sure everything was above board he was completely reassured.'

'Dad did that?' Portia's gentle heart swelled with love and gratitude. 'He really did check up for me?'

'Of course. We're not complete monsters.'

'Oh.' It was all she could manage to say; she

couldn't stop smiling. Deep down her parents did care about her, and little Sam, and that meant so much to her that she didn't mind in the least being hustled down the short garden path to where a sedately gleaming Daimler was parked, its chauffeur already stowing all her despised luggage in the boot.

Even when Lucenzo loomed over her, his strong, lean face tight with displeasure, his dark eyes brilliant and incisive, she couldn't wipe the beam of happiness from her face.

'Get in,' he ordered coldly, indicating the rear of the opulent car, taking the cot from her unresisting hands. Sucking in a shallow breath, he lifted the warm, shawl-wrapped bundle in careful hands and strapped the sleeping child in the car-seat.

At eight weeks Vittorio's son had lost that crumpled new look; now he looked smooth and adorable, his shock of raven-dark hair proclaiming his heritage.

His heart lurched unexpectedly. Vittorio's child.

If his half-brother had been a faithful, responsible husband then this baby would have been Lorna's, and he would have welcomed the new generation of his family with pride and joy. As it was...

Sliding along the leather upholstery, Portia watched those long, elegantly boned fingers deal with the complicated-looking arrangement of straps. Then her eyes lifted to his face, intent on what he was doing. His incredibly thick and dark lashes cast pools of shadow against the olive-toned skin of his high, arrogant cheekbones and his mouth, passionate and sensual, was tight with concentration. He really was utterly gorgeous, she thought as a weird inner quiver made her mouth run dry. Something about the hard sweep of his wide shoulders encased in the finest tailoring made her think of male protectiveness as well as the domination she instinctively expected from him.

As he finished his task his dark eyes lifted to meet her fascinated gaze, and something strange shivered down her spine and curled wickedly in the pit of her stomach. Her softly curved mouth fell open as she struggled for breath, her eyes widening helplessly as she tried to come to terms with the unthinkable. She was being turned on by an arrogant pig who thought she was a cheap slag, not fit to be seen around his exalted family!

Huge eyes that had turned to shimmering liquid silver watched with mindless fixity as his dark gaze assimilated the hot colour she felt flood her face, the way her breath came in tiny anguished spurts, making her breasts lift and peak provocatively. Watched that long, beautiful mouth curl cynically down at one corner before he moved away, closing the car door with a decisive clunk and turning to speak to her parents.

Hardly knowing which was worse, her embarrassment or her humiliation, Portia knotted her hands together and stared rigidly ahead. She was unaware that they were actually moving, that she hadn't properly said farewell to her parents, until she registered that Lucenzo Verdi had taken the driver's seat, with the uniformed chauffeur sitting stiffly at his side.

Squashing her juvenile impulse to shriek, Stop this car! she turned her attention to her sleeping baby, rearranging the folds of his shawl to steady herself, to wipe away the memory of how she'd felt when Lucenzo's dark eyes had clashed with hers.

She soon became absorbed in little Sam as his rosebud mouth curved in a windy smile. He was so perfect, from the top of his downy head to his tiny, tiny toenails! They were together, that was the most important thing, embarking on an adventure. And she, as his doting mother, would ensure that nothing happened to separate them. Ever!

At least the biggest fly in the ointment would take himself off to find more congenial company just as soon as he had delivered them to Sam's Italian grandfather. She couldn't wait!

Lifting her head, she met his glance in the rearview mirror and quickly looked away, her face going pink as she felt the thunder of blood at her pulse-points. She didn't know what was happening here, but whatever it was she didn't like it. She couldn't be sexually aware of him—attracted—she *couldn't*!

She stared fixedly out of the window at her side. The way a person looked had never cut much ice with her; it was what was inside that mattered. In fact, she had never really thought about Vito's pretty-boy goodlooks, having been more impressed by what she had been conned into believing was his determination to make good.

She sighed mournfully. And to cap it all the English early summer was living up to its not always deserved reputation. Raindrops were sliding down the glass like teardrops…

Lucenzo activated the windscreen wipers, concentrating on the airport approach. She was still smiling, he thought grittily. She had hardly stopped since she'd approached the car, safe in the knowledge that her dreams of getting her hands on as much as she could wrest from the bulging coffers of the Verdi family were about to become reality.

Except for that time when he'd glanced up from securing Vittorio's baby in the car-seat and found her watching him with what he had only been able to interpret as blatant sexual invitation.

Was that the way she'd looked at Vittorio? A pink flush on her cheeks, her eyes eating him up, her soft lips parted, her breath coming in rapid little pants? Was that how it had happened—just one look? His half-brother wouldn't have turned down such an offer.

Two hours later the private jet was airborne. Lucenzo, his long legs stretched out in front of him, extracted a sheaf of papers from his briefcase and tried to concentrate, to shut out the presence of the female at his side.

But that was proving difficult while she was playing with the baby who was gurgling back at her. And today she looked different from when he'd first seen her six weeks ago. Not so bunchy-looking now, in clean but well-worn jeans and a plain white T-shirt, her hair shining with health and caught into her nape with a scarlet ribbon.

Better, but in his jaded experience still not the type the unfaithful Vittorio had been constitutionally unable to resist—he had liked glitz and glamour, trophy women. But something had drawn him to this one. Perhaps, he thought as the flight attendant approached with a feeding bottle, perhaps it was the smile.

It was radiant as she took the bottle, lighting up her otherwise unremarkable face, and her voice was soft and lilting as she answered the attendant's, 'I hope it's not too hot?'

'It's just right—and thank you so much. It's very kind of you!'

Butter wouldn't melt, Lucenzo thought sourly, trying to blot out the sound of the two women admiring his half-brother's baby. The child looked contented and well cared for, and as far as he could tell she appeared to be a good mother. But then, he reminded himself cynically as his eyes were reluctantly drawn to the gentle hand that caressed the baby's soft cheek as he hungrily suckled, Vittorio's son was her trump card, her passport to the Verdi wealth. No wonder she treated him as though he were the most precious thing on earth.

Sighing irritably, he rustled his papers and answered the flight attendant's offer of coffee with a terse negative.

As the other girl moved away Portia decided she had to do something about this tense state of affairs. She didn't mind for herself, but the spiky atmosphere couldn't be good for little Sam. Hadn't she read somewhere that even tiny babies could pick up vibes and be affected by them?

'I've never flown before,' she confided, to start the

conversational ball rolling, casting him a wary smile. This not-speaking business was ridiculous. He'd made his dislike of her obvious, but surely they could be polite to each other? The only words he'd said to her had been icy orders, telling her where to go and what to do.

She lifted Sam and laid him against her shoulder, gently rubbing his back. She'd pretend the disapproving Lucenzo Verdi was an ordinary human being, just another fellow traveller. She'd always enjoyed talking to people.

From where she was sitting that wasn't going to be too easy. The expression on his austerely handsome profile would have done a hanging judge proud. Even so, she launched out cheerfully, 'When I was growing up my parents took me for improving holidays. Museums, art galleries, sites of historical interest—they didn't believe in lying in the sun on Mediterranean beaches. Then, when I was earning for myself and they'd thrown in the towel when it came to improving me, I didn't take holidays. I just saved all I could for—'

Her cheeks going fiery red, Portia stopped herself just in time. She'd been babbling. Her mother always said she never thought before she opened her mouth. It really wouldn't do to tell him she'd been saving for what she had always dreamed of: a wedding, a home of her own and children. That after she'd met and fallen in love with Vito she'd redoubled her efforts, believing him when he'd said they'd marry as soon as it was financially possible.

Lucenzo probably missed his brother dreadfully, still mourned his untimely death, she thought compassionately. She was not going to rub in the fact that Vito had been a liar and a cheat. She wasn't into hurting people, even if they were patronising beasts.

He didn't seem to notice that her torrent had broken off mid-sentence; he appeared to be intent on what he was reading. But his eyes weren't moving. Those fabulous lashes were making inky shadows against the harshly beautiful line of his cheekbones.

Asleep? No way. She'd never seen a pair of shoulders look less relaxed.

Pointedly ignoring her? Most certainly. Her soft mouth twitched. It wouldn't do the wretched man any harm to unbend a little. 'I think he's just about to drop off,' she imparted chirpily, meaning Sam, who was lying in her arms, his little arms stretched above his head, his eyelids drooping.

No response. But Portia wasn't ready to give up yet. Surely he didn't intend to spend the whole of the flight in this forbidding silence? There were things she wanted to know about the family she was about to meet, the place she was expected to inhabit for goodness only knew how long—a week, a month, a year?

This darkly handsome, coldly unresponsive persona surely wasn't all there was to this man. Someone, somewhere, must see the other, more human side?

'Are you married, Lucenzo? Do you have a family?' she asked impulsively.

People he loved, who loved him back? Children he played with who knew how he looked when he threw back his head and laughed at their antics? A wife who saw melting adoration in those dark, hostile eyes, who knew every inch of that lithe and powerful body...?

Portia swallowed painfully, the now all-too familiar frisson of intense excitement taking her breath away, accelerating her heartbeat. She shouldn't be thinking that way, picturing him naked, with desire softening his mouth, heating his eyes. Imagining what it would be like to be held in his arms...

She'd never indulged in erotic fantasies, not ever, she thought with growing alarm. The inclination simply hadn't been there, not even with Vito. Or the couple of boyfriends she'd had before him. Their interest in her had fizzled out rapidly after they'd met her parents and come up against the brick wall of their restrictions.

Her mother had warned her. 'Always remember, most men are only after one thing. It takes brains and looks to attract the honourable attentions of a man of the right calibre.' And she had neither brains nor looks. That had been the implication.

Confused and miserable, Portia glared at the fluffy blanket of clouds which was all she could see out of the window, wishing she was anywhere in the world but here.

Sliding the papers back into his briefcase, Lucenzo glanced at her. So she wanted to talk, did she? A nice chatty little dialogue to while away the time? She was too self-absorbed and thick-skinned to take on board the fact that the last thing he wanted was idle conversation with a husband-stealer who was the next best thing to a blackmailer.

So he'd talk, and she'd only have herself to blame if she didn't like what he had to say.

Ignoring her question about his marital status, because she, of all people, had no damned right to pry into that painful part of his life—any part of his life, if it came to that—he drawled silkily, 'Your parents seemed glad to be rid of you. No fond farewells, no promises to phone or write. I wonder why?'

He could well imagine, he thought drily as he watched what had to be guilty colour steal over her face. She'd probably been trouble since the day she was born. Feckless, irresponsible, with an eye for the main chance.

Mindful of the bad atmosphere that could affect her baby, Portia swallowed an angry retort. Besides, if she'd viewed their parting from where he'd been standing she might have jumped to that conclusion.

Always ready to extend the benefit of the doubt, she turned to face him, explaining softly and earnestly, 'You mustn't think badly of them—'

'I assure you, it is not them I'm condemning,' he interjected sardonically.

Only her, Portia recognised on a muted sigh. Par for the course. Nevertheless, she didn't want to leave him with the impression that her parents didn't care about her, because they did.

'They're both getting on a bit—they married late and I came as a surprise. They can't afford to keep me and little Sam, and if I went back to work I couldn't afford to pay for childcare so it would be down to them. They can't cope with the thought of having to look after—' she recalled her mother's exact words on the subject '—a squalling baby who would grow into a rumbustious toddler, a clumsy schoolboy and in all likelihood a problem teenager. Not that he would, of course, and he never squalls,' she denied breathlessly. 'But you can see their point. They want peace in their declining years. Of course they saw your father's offer to have me and Sam live with him as the only sensible way out of the situation. Even so, they cared enough to contact your father and—'

'And find out exactly what was on offer,' Lucenzo interjected tightly. 'This I know. My father's integrity and misguided generosity was questioned. I find that offensive. And don't try to tell me that you didn't jump at the opportunity.'

Portia chewed on her lip as she desperately tried to decide how to answer that.

His black eyes were full of hostile reproach, she noted uncomfortably. If he saw her father's natural parental concern as an affront to the precious dignity of his family then what would he think if she blurted out the truth? How could she possibly tell him that accepting his father's 'misguidedly generous' invitation had been the last thing she'd wanted? That only her parents' pushing, nagging and much vaunted logic had made her reluctantly accept it?

It didn't bear thinking about.

And what sort of family was she going to, anyway? Horrible doubts assailed her all over again. They were wealthy, they were powerful, they thought they were better than anyone else. And if they were like Lucenzo they would regard her as scum, would only want Vito's son, intent only on forcing her to agree to give him up.

Sheer fright made her blurt, 'It's OK for your father to see Sam—well, I'd be a fool if I didn't think that. They are related. But if I'm not satisfied I can leave whenever I want and take Sam with me.'

It hadn't come out as she'd meant it to. She'd been scared, on the defensive. She hadn't meant to sound so—so confrontational.

Too late now to retract. His beautiful eyes had narrowed to slits of black ice, his fabulous bone structure going tight with what she could only assume to be disgust.

'I think we should get a few things straight,' Lucenzo said with a chilling bite. That sweetness and light, slightly scatty act was just that. An act. She'd just opened her mouth and confirmed every last one of his opinions. If she wasn't satisfied, getting everything she expected, she would threaten to take his father's grandson away from him.

His mouth turned down at one corner as he scanned her flushed face, the softly trembling lips, her wide, stricken eyes. 'You can cut the injured innocent act; we both know you're neither,' he imparted harshly. 'Did you get pregnant on purpose to give you a hold on the family? No—don't bother to answer that,' he said impatiently as her mouth dropped open. 'It's irrelevant now.'

He sucked in a breath. If she could make threats he could go one better. 'I practically begged my father to have nothing to do with you, apart from making adequate financial provision for Vittorio's son. But he was adamant, and because he's a sick man I reluctantly went along with his wishes to bring you and the child to him. And one word—one whisper—out of you with regard to taking his grandson away from him and you will feel the full might of the Verdi family come down on you. We will fight you for custody and you will leave with nothing. This I promise.'

CHAPTER THREE

LEMON trees in terracotta pots marched along the terrace fronting the imposing Villa Fontebella, and wisteria hanging in soft blue clouds festooned the white marble columns that supported the long, shade-giving arcade.

As the driver of the limo which had ferried them from the airport opened the door at her side Portia took a deep breath and reluctantly slid out. She stood on legs that were shaking so much they would barely hold her upright.

The awesome villa, with its backdrop of thickly wooded hills, was set in formal Florentine gardens overlooking breathtaking views of sweeps of vines and olive trees, right over the rooftops of tiny villages clustered round ancient churches and down to the silver loop of a river far below. It was the sort of place only the seriously wealthy inhabited.

Portia gulped, agitation making her eyes dark in the now ashen pallor of her face. Not even the warm Italian sun could take away the shivers that came from the very core of her being. Ever since Lucenzo had made that truly terrifying threat, as good as accusing her of entrapping Vito for what she hoped to gain, she'd been panicking inside, feeling colder and sicker with every mile of progress into the unknown.

The silence that had descended after he'd given her that dreadful warning had been almost tangible. She could have reached out and touched it if she'd had the nerve.

As she put shaky fingers to her throbbing temples she heard Sam begin to grizzle and made a determined effort to pull herself together. Ignoring Lucenzo, who was overseeing the unloading of her despised and multitudinous belongings from the boot of the car, its driver passing them to a burly man in a cool white jacket, she scrambled back inside the vehicle, blinking away threatening tears.

Little Sam was hungry, his legs kicking wildly, one tiny fist thrust into his mouth. Doing her best to make cheerful soothing noises, she scrabbled ineffectually with the straps of the car-seat while Sam's face went red with rage and his grizzles turned into full-throated roars.

'I'll have you out in a moment, sweetheart,' Portia promised with blatant over-optimism, struggling to keep the wobble of desperate misery out of her voice as she tugged at a clasp that seemed to have been welded shut.

'Let me.' The door nearest the car-seat opened and Lucenzo dealt with the enigma of the safety straps in seconds, lifting the fretful baby in capable hands and holding him against his shoulder.

Miraculously, Sam stopped crying immediately, and, sitting back on her heels and blinking ferociously, Portia saw her precious son nuzzle his face into Lucenzo's neck. She was utterly and unwillingly transfixed by the smile that transformed the austerity of the Italian's features into sheer, stunning male beauty.

Her heart lurched so madly she felt breathless, dizzy and disorientated. Lucenzo had never smiled for her. Not once. With a peculiar little ache in the region of her now pattering heart she wished he would. And felt her face flare with hot colour.

Was she completely stupid, or something? As feather-brained as her parents had always despairingly said she was? Of course he wouldn't smile at her like that. Lucenzo Verdi wouldn't give her the time of day if he could avoid it. He thought she was the dregs.

Wriggling backwards out of the rear seat, she told herself to get real. Lucenzo Verdi was her enemy; he had made that plain from the very start. She mustn't let her wits wander off into fantasy. She had to keep them on red alert if she were to have any hope of handling the impossibly autocratic Italian. She could only hope the rest of Vito's family weren't cast in the same condemnatory mould.

Hanging on to the bodywork of the car, she went to reclaim her baby—and even though her legs felt like jelly her chin was high as she reached up for him.

But Lucenzo raked his dark eyes comprehensively over her pale features, her tear-spiked lashes and drooping mouth, and relayed tonelessly, 'I'll carry him in. You look on the point of collapse.'

And whose fault was that? Portia inwardly fulminated as he turned to face the house, Sam, now blowing happy bubbles, held high in his arms, and strode over the immaculately raked gravel towards open double doors.

Like a victor triumphantly returning with the spoils of war, Portia thought sickeningly, urging herself to keep up with his long-legged stride, resisting the fraught impulse to hammer her fists against that broad back and demand he hand her baby back to her.

In a flurry of now breathless agitation Portia tripped over her feet as she scurried in his wake up the sweeping stone steps, and she felt something clench sharply inside her, taking what was left of her breath away, as Lucenzo put his free hand out to steady her and said grimly, 'There's no need to bust a gut. You'll get your feet under the table soon enough.'

She simply couldn't wait, could she? he thought edgily. His mouth settled into a hard straight line as he steadied her, then hauled her round to face him. But it softened unconsciously as he registered the pallor of her weary face, the tiny beads of perspiration on her short upper lip, the soft trembling of her mouth and the defeated droop of her shoulders.

Somewhere along the line she'd lost her ribbon, and now her shimmering golden hair fell around her shoulders, tendrils curving around her throat, wisps falling across those wide grey eyes.

Santa Maria! She looked done in, he thought with a stab of unwilling compassion. She obviously wasn't strong, and maybe—just maybe—that fainting fit at Vittorio's funeral hadn't been an act. And maybe, heaven forbid, she was about to give a repeat performance.

His grip on her arm gentled, became supportive rather than punitive, as he suggested, 'Get some rest. You can meet the family in the morning. I'll show you to your room—Alfredo has taken your things up, and I'll send Assunta to you. Don't worry, she looked after me and Vittorio when we were small so she knows what she's doing. Plus, she speaks fluent English.'

As they passed into the hall he felt her body sag. He sucked in a breath, wondering if she was about to pass out, and instinctively wrapped his free arm around her surprisingly neat waist, supporting her against the length of his own body.

Anyone seeing them like this would think he actually cared about the blackmailing little tramp, when all he was desperate to do was get her to her room, leave Assunta to deal with her and wash his hands of her and her greedy machinations.

With a heartfelt sigh Portia leant against him, overwhelmed, her eyes filling with stupid tears. Just one gesture of kindness and she was willing to forgive and forget everything, wanting to cling onto him, wrap her arms around him and beg him to be her friend.

How pathetic could she get? she asked herself on a tidal wave of self-disgust. And to cap it all the sheer opulence of her surroundings—the costly antiques, the sweeping marble staircase, the porcelain bowls of flowers on every available surface—shook her rigid. What on earth did she think she was doing in a place like this? The nearest thing to an antique in her parents' home was her grandmother's brass jam kettle!

'Can you manage the stairs?' Lucenzo asked with

level politeness, biting back his distaste for the whole situation. 'Or shall I find someone to help you?'

As it was, Vittorio's baby was squirming vigorously, grabbing handfuls of his hair and tugging with surprising strength for something so small, and if Portia collapsed halfway up she could well fall all the way back again before he could do anything about it. A dark frisson of the soul almost paralysed him at the thought of that, and he took a deep breath as he waited for it to pass.

Then he gritted his teeth, blocking out the memory, looking for the nearest chair to park her on. He could understand why there wasn't a welcoming committee. His father would be resting, obeying his doctor's and his own strict instructions, and his aunts and his sister-in-law wouldn't be straining at the leash to come face to face with the evidence of Vittorio's infidelity.

At least, he consoled himself, he'd kept the worst of it from his family. They didn't know that the infidelity had been the serial kind.

'Of course I can manage.' Portia pushed some backbone into her voice and with a reluctance that appalled her, and a feeling inside her that was verging on pain, pulled away from his supporting arm, the heated strength of his body. Very deliberately she put space between them, when all she really wanted to do was to lean against him, borrow strength from his lean and powerful body.

It had been so long since she'd been held she'd forgotten how comforting it could be. Displays of affection had always embarrassed her parents and not

even Vito, whom she'd loved, had made her feel so—
so safe. And had her senses ever reacted so instinctively to Vito? Had she felt this sensual pull at his
maleness?

'No!' She hadn't realised she'd spoken aloud in
fraught denial of the way this man who was her enemy
could make her feel. The father of her child hadn't
come near to making it seem as if the world was spinning around her, leaving her out of control.

'What is it?' Lucenzo gave her a spearing glance
from beneath lowered brows. At least she had some
colour now. A bright wash of it stained her cheeks,
and her grey eyes were huge, glittering with something
that looked like the panic of a cornered young animal.

'N-nothing—' Flustered, she pushed her hands
through her hair, dragging it away from her face, then
sucked in a breath. Lucenzo's eyes were held by the
resulting thrust of her breasts, the nipples proud and
prominent against the thin fabric of her top.

Frowning, he dragged his eyes away, and a split
second later Portia was leaping up the staircase, hanging on to the wrought-iron banister. Settling Vittorio's
child more securely in his arms, Lucenzo followed—
and found his eyes annoyingly glued to Portia's neat
and curvy denim-clad backside.

Five foot four of lushly delineated curves, shimmering blonde hair, lips like ripe cherries and that
breathless, though obviously spurious air of ingenu-
ousness—was that what had tempted his half-brother
away from his wife, his normally ultra-elegant bits on
the side?

Disliking the road his thoughts were taking him down, he quickened his steps and caught up with her at the head of the sweeping staircase, where the upper hall gave onto corridors branching in three directions.

'This way,' he instructed tautly. He didn't look at her. He didn't want to connect with those wide, seemingly vulnerable eyes, recognise that elusive nameless something that had captivated his half-brother. He simply strode ahead.

Portia followed, feeling unwanted and seriously unnecessary, wishing she'd never agreed to come here. When he paused by one of the carved oak doors that lined the seemingly endless corridor and flung it open, telling her tightly, 'Your suite of rooms,' she felt a deep and dreadful reluctance to cross the threshold.

'I want to go home.'

The childishly wailed words were out before she could swallow them and she cringed with supercharged embarrassment, reddening hectically as he remarked witheringly, 'If that's your opening salvo, forget it.'

Vulnerable? How could he have thought that for one insane moment? Portia Makepeace was about as vulnerable as an armoured car!

He reminded her stonily, 'I've told you what will happen if you threaten to do anything to upset my father. Here—' He placed Sam in her arms and took a backward pace, as if the air she breathed out was full of pestilence and plague. 'Make Vittorio's son comfortable. I will send Assunta to you to make sure you are behaving as my father would wish.'

Holding her baby close to her heart, gathering much needed strength from the adored warm little body, Portia blurted, 'I didn't come here to be kept under house arrest! I came because your father wants to see his grandson. So when can I meet him?'

Her chin came up, even though her voice held a disgraceful wobble. She was sick of being treated like dirt, ordered around. Her future relationship with Sam's grandfather was all that counted. Lucenzo's low opinion of her shouldn't matter, but it did hurt, she acknowledged sickly, more than she knew it should.

'Tomorrow,' he told her curtly. 'I will let him know that Vittorio's son has arrived safely. For tonight that will be enough. As I have already told you, my father is a sick man.'

Watching him stride away, Portia felt her heart plummet to new depths, her mouth going dry. How sick was sick? Eduardo Verdi had sounded so kind in that letter he'd written her. He'd come across as being someone she could talk to with the ease and openness that came so naturally to her.

All through her nightmare journey she'd been counting on him as head of the family to intercede on her behalf, to perhaps persuade Lucenzo that she wasn't as downright bad as he thought she was.

Portia shuddered, immediately hating herself for such selfish, unworthy thoughts. If the poor old man was ill then the most she could hope for was that see-ing and holding his new little grandson would make him feel a whole lot better!

She could stand up for herself where Lucenzo was

concerned, of course she could. And one day, if he stayed around, she would force him to listen to her side of the story—even if, as he'd clearly demonstrated, he had no wish to hear it.

And when she met Eduardo she would do nothing, say nothing to upset or tire him. Of course she wouldn't.

Annoyingly, her eyes pickled with compassionate tears. She blinked them rapidly away and forced herself to carry her now restless Sam over the threshold and into the most beautiful bedroom she'd ever seen.

No time to take stock, except to note that her luggage, looking even tattier against a backdrop of unnerving opulence, was in an ungainly heap at the foot of a four-poster which was trigged out with the most fantastic cream-coloured gauzy drapes.

Chattering consolingly to the baby, who was squirming in the crook of her left arm, she eventually located the changing mat, nappies and a fresh Babygro, scattering items not wanted at the moment over the soft blue carpet until she saw two shiny black shoes planted in the middle of the mayhem she'd created.

Lifting her eyes above the level of the black flatties, she encountered thick black stockings, a pristine grey overall and a cheerful round face surmounted by dark, grey-streaked frizzily permed hair.

Portia swallowed noisily. 'Assunta?'

Friend or foe?

'I did knock but you did not hear.'

Which wasn't surprising, considering the racket

Sam was making, Portia thought, eyeing the older woman warily.

Her heart surged with relief when Assunta beamed widely. '*Tanto bello!* What is all this noise about, little one? May I hold him?'

At Portia's tongue-tied nod Assunta swept Sam up into her arms, clucking over him, 'People say all babies look the same, but that isn't true. This little one is just like his father and I should know. I looked after him from when he was born until his mother took him back to England when he was five years old. Mind you, he did spend his holidays here with his father; Signor Eduardo insisted on that. Now, shall we make the little one comfortable? This way—I will show you. We have everything ready.'

Snatching up everything she needed, Portia followed as Assunta marched through one of the two connecting doors and into a light and airy nursery that looked as if it had been designed by experts. Expensive experts.

'I need to make up his bottle.' Portia cut into the older woman's explanation of where everything was, anxiously aware that it was well past Sam's feed time, that his routine was going to pot, and got a straight look, a beat of silence.

'Of course.'

Was that condemnation, disappointment in Assunta's dark eyes? At that moment Portia neither knew nor cared, and practically sprinted across the room when the other woman indicated an alcove fitted with a work surface, stainless steel sink, electric kettle and sterilising equipment. Someone had thought of everything.

'We did not know whether the child was breast or bottle fed. Now—' a lighter tone, quite definitely lighter '—shall I change him while you do that?'

Suppressing maternal possessiveness, Portia murmured her thanks. While the kettle boiled she confided sadly, 'I did so want to feed him myself, but I got this infection. It was a really awful time.' Not just the pain, or the fever, though that had been bad enough, but the feeling she was failing her newborn. That had been the very worst part. 'Then, when it had cleared up—'

Her huge grey eyes glistened with retrospective tears. Her mother always said she lived too near the waterworks, and her mother, as always, was right. Portia sniffed, wishing she wasn't so over-emotional, and finished the job of cooling the bottle under the cold water tap.

When she was settled in the nursing chair Assunta plonked down comfortably on the wide windowseat and told her warmly, 'You mustn't blame yourself. These things happen. You are a good mother—I have seen poor ones, so I know the difference. You do your best for your son; I can see that.'

Portia beamed ecstatically. It was the first nice thing anyone had said to her in days! The way Assunta had said 'your son', instead of Lucenzo's repressive 'Vittorio's son', as if she herself were some sort of regrettable afterthought, warmed her heart.

And she knew the Italian woman was on her side when she admitted, on a sigh of contentment, 'It is good to have a baby in the house again after all this time. Vito's mother took him away when he was barely five years old, and Lucenzo had already been sent away to school by then. Poor little mite. Christine, Vito's mother, had been originally hired to teach Lucenzo English. Signor Verdi wished his son to grow up bilingual. But she set her cap at him—Signor Verdi, that is—and they were married. When Vito was born Signora Christine insisted that Lucenzo was sent away to school; he was only six years old.'

Which made him thirty-two now, Portia thought, struggling with her mental arithmetic. 'Vito's mother wanted him to be the most important child in the house?' she guessed, her tender heart melting for the poor, banished little boy.

'But of course.' Assunta's round face set into lines of disapproval. 'She had very little time for her baby, but he was her stake in the Verdi fortune. After the birth she had no time for her husband, either—only for spending his money and flirting with other men. After the divorce she returned to England with what she wanted—a fat settlement. I'm sure she would have left little Vito behind, but his father insisted the child needed his mother.'

She gave a sigh that came up from the soles of her sensible black shoes. 'Poor Vito might have made a better marriage if he hadn't used his mercenary, cold-hearted mother as a blueprint. Even if he hadn't met you and fallen in love his marriage wouldn't have lasted. But you'll know all about that. Such a tragedy.' Her eyes filled with tears and Portia felt her own water in sympathy. 'For him to be killed before he could make you his wife. You must have loved each other very much. And I want you to know—' she sniffed loudly, struggling with emotion '—whatever the family thinks, I'm here for you.'

Oh, heavens above! Portia scrubbed at her own brimming eyes as she gasped sincerely, 'Thank you, Assunta. I do appreciate that.'

She lifted Sam against her shoulder to de-burp him. Assunta was one very nice lady and had obviously doted on Vito. How could she tell her that Vito had never loved her, had lied to her more times than most people had had hot dinners? She simply couldn't do it!

Wanting to change the potentially awkward subject, she said the first thing that came into her head, asking, 'What happened to Lucenzo's mother? And was he dreadfully upset when he was sent away to school when he was so young?'

It seemed really right to focus on Lucenzo. Instinctive, but puzzling, too. Hopefully Assunta would put the change of subject down to her unwillingness to be upset by talking about the father of her child, when the truth was that she was, oddly, far more interested in Lucenzo.

Her cheeks warm, Portia rose and laid the sleepy baby in the cot—a wonderful confection of pale blue muslin and ivory-coloured lace and far more sumptuous than anything she could ever have afforded—to cover her discomfiture. Just why did Lucenzo occupy her mind so much? It wasn't sensible and it probably wasn't natural. So why did it feel as if it was?

'That was another tragedy,' Assunta sighed. Already back on her feet, she was rinsing out Sam's bottle, and elaborated through billowing clouds of steam. 'Lucenzo was just three months old when his mother died of some rare viral infection, so he never knew her. By the time Vittorio was born he was completely self-contained. If he was unhappy at being sent away to school he didn't show it, not even to me,' she confided sorrowfully. 'Ever since Christine got Signor Eduardo where she wanted him she'd been doing her best to push little Lucenzo into the background. I saw it happen with my own eyes. But even then Lucenzo was too proud to show his feelings.'

Assunta turned, wiping her capable hands on the towel that hung from a hoop above the stainless steel sink at the business end of the nursery. 'I'm not telling you all this for the sake of it. You should understand about this family if you are to be a part of it. There have been too many tragedies. So if the family is cold towards you—most especially Lucenzo, because he has not been the same since what happened to his wife—it is because they are still trying to come to terms with Vittorio's death.'

Portia's mouth dropped open and she blinked rapidly. Disregarding the bit about the family's possible coldness because she had more or less expected something of the sort—except from Sam's grandfather—she grappled with the unwelcome information that Lucenzo was married, scowling slightly because she couldn't lie to herself and pretend it wasn't unwelcome.

And what exactly had happened with his wife? Had she, like his stepmother, done a runner? About to ask, she felt the words die in her throat as Lucenzo strode through the nursery door, his narrowed eyes lancing between the two now silent women as if he knew they'd been talking about him.

He'd changed into a cream-coloured light jacket and narrow dark trousers and looked so detachedly handsome that Portia could only stare at him, feeling oddly light-headed.

When his black eyes turned back to her and settled she could scarcely breathe, and could think of nothing at all to say when he told her with flat formality, 'My father wants to see you. I suggest you make yourself presentable. I will return to take you to him in ten minutes. I don't expect you to keep him waiting.'

CHAPTER FOUR

TEN minutes!

Her feet firmly glued to the cream-coloured nursery carpet, Portia widened her eyes at the spot where Lucenzo had been standing, her heart thumping beneath her breastbone.

She had been summoned.

Unnervingly, she felt as if she'd just received a royal command. Should she practise her curtsey? It certainly felt like it! And was she supposed to take Sam along with her? Lucenzo hadn't mentioned him, though introducing Sam to his grandfather was the only reason she'd been invited here. But the little darling was sleeping; she really didn't want to disturb him—

Assunta settled the matter with innate practicality. 'I'll stay with the little one until you get back. I can make myself comfortable in your sitting room and send down for a tray, so don't worry yourself about us.' Her mouth curved wryly as she prodded gently, 'Don't you think you should hurry?'

Portia conceded she should, but she moved reluctantly out of the nursery, her feet dragging. She hated the way Lucenzo issued his orders and made threats—some veiled, some right out in the open. Do this—don't do that—or else!

54

It was the 'or else' bit that made her blood run cold—the knowledge that if she put a foot wrong he would do his damnedest to make his father agree that they could do without the likes of her to sully the family name, and move heaven and earth to take her baby from her.

They could afford the best lawyers money could buy, clever men who would blow her rights and objections clear out of the water.

Apparently Assunta had seen nothing wrong in the way he'd spoken to her. Italian women pampered their menfolk from the cradle to the grave; in their eyes they could do no wrong.

But ten minutes? She needed an hour at least before she could make herself look anything like presentable! She needed a shower to sluice away the stickiness of the long hours of travelling and she hadn't even begun to unpack.

Portia shrugged fatalistically and pulled a mutinous face at her less than pristine person in one of the ornately framed mirrors that reflected the gauzily hung four-poster back at her.

A quick wash and brush-up would have to suffice; she hadn't been given time to find something more suitable than these old jeans and her baby-dribbled T-shirt to wear, had she?

The *en suite* bathroom made her eyes pop. Good grief, the sunken marble bath was big enough to swim in, the walls were floor-to-ceiling mirrors and there were enough classy bottles and jars displayed on the floating glass shelves to stock Harrods' perfumery department!

Feeling disturbingly out of her depth again, Portia hurriedly washed her face and grabbed the nearest towel. Still rubbing the moisture off her skin, she padded back to her bedroom to root in the depths of her handbag for a comb. She was dragging it through her hair when, after a decidedly perfunctory tap, Lucenzo walked through the door.

Did he have to look so sternly forbidding? Portia thought as her stomach flew up to her throat and zoomed back down again. Coupled with all that raw sexuality it was almost too much to take! It was like looking at a mouthwatering cream cake and knowing that the tempting confection hid a lethal poison!

Dropping the comb back into the cluttered depths of her bag, she gulped in air and strove for a bright, friendly tone. 'I'm ready.' But it came out all wrong, husky and breathy, and made her feel completely silly.

'You intend to meet my father looking like that?' His beautiful mouth essayed something that to Portia markedly resembled a sneer—although, to be fair, it could be impatience, she decided charitably. She smartly changed her mind when he added, 'You mean to grace the dinner table looking like a pauper so that Father will feel sorry for you and double your dress allowance?'

Grace the dinner table? Oh, help! And what dress allowance? She hadn't asked for any such thing! How dared he suggest she expected one?

Angry colour began to flood her face. 'Do you know

something?' she ground out through tightly clenched teeth. 'I hate you. I really do!' And she absolutely meant it. She who had never before hated a single living soul loathed Lucenzo Verdi with a passion that amazed her into momentary silence.

But, seeing the way his upper lip curled, dark brows shifting slightly upwards, she blustered on indignantly, 'You gave me—no, you ordered me to be ready in ten minutes! I haven't unpacked yet, so how can I possibly have had time to change?'

'Paolina has unpacked for you,' he delivered coolly, unfazed by her blistering outburst, and strode over to an enormous hanging cupboard which boasted heavy oak doors carved with impossibly stout cherubs, swags of vines, peacocks and fantastic flowers.

Portia swallowed jerkily, her hand going up to her throat. She'd been too flustered to notice that the muddle she'd created on the floor had been tidied away and that her suitcase was missing. Her meagre belongings were now lost in the cavernous depths he exposed, and as his fingers sorted through the very few occupied hangers she had an awful sinking feeling inside her, knowing what must be coming next.

That truly awful dress.

She'd made it herself, when seized by a misguided and short-lived enthusiasm for home dressmaking, and was convinced there'd been something wrong with the pattern or the instructions—or both. There had to have been for the end result to look so dreadful.

Her normal wardrobe consisted of jeans and tops, with just a couple of flowery skirts for when the weather turned summery. Her mother had said, 'Charity shop trousers might be all right for slopping around at home but they won't cut the mustard at an Italian millionaire's villa! This is the only dress you own; you'll have to take it.'

Portia wished she'd burned it months ago as Lucenzo advanced. Hanging over his arm, it didn't look too bad. The fabric was crisp and fresh, a nice saxe-blue dotted with oyster-coloured swirls, but when it was on…

How he would wish he hadn't forced her to wear it, she decided wickedly, a sudden mutinous gleam in her eyes as she reached for it, her fingers tangling in the folds of material as she turned, heading for the bathroom.

'No, you don't,' Lucenzo breathed, catching her by the shoulders and dragging her round to face him. 'It takes normal women hours to change so it will probably take you days, out of sheer perversity! Dinner will be served in half an hour and Father wants a private meeting with you beforehand. Already we are keeping him waiting.'

His spectacular eyes were narrowed with impatience and Portia could only stare at him, unwillingly mesmerised by the way the evening sunlight streamed through the many tall windows and glistened on his soft midnight hair, moulding the aesthetic perfection of his intimidatingly masculine features.

She could see the way a lock of his expertly barbered hair tumbled rebelliously over his wide forehead, the tiny frown line between his slashing brows, the thick sweep of dark lashes, the strong line of his patrician nose and the infinitely fascinating and shatteringly sensual curve of his lower lip.

It was such a shame that what went on inside his head and in his heart—if he had one—didn't match the perfect exterior, she thought mournfully. She unconsciously laved her suddenly parched lips, then gave a feeble yelp of outrage as he took the hem of her T-shirt and dragged it over her head.

'How dare you?' Portia wailed as soon as she could retrieve the breath that had seemed to be securely locked in her lungs during the timeless moments when his veiled eyes had travelled over all her exposed flesh.

She was cringingly aware of the shortcomings of her plain white cotton bra. It was too small. She'd put on quite a bit of weight in that department during her pregnancy and she knew she positively billowed...

She made a desperate lunge for the despised and despicable garment still draped over his arm, sniping out, 'I don't know what you think you're doing.'

As her head disappeared into the folds she wondered why she should harbour the utterly wanton wish that his hands had followed the quite blatant track of his eyes.

Maybe she'd been born wicked as well as stupid!

Lucenzo sucked a breath through his teeth, backing off a pace and turning quickly away as her flushed face and tousled hair emerged. Her arms flailed as she found the sleeves of this dress that had been hanging between a shabby raincoat and a couple of limp-looking skirts.

'I am trying to hurry proceedings along,' he answered, forcing a lazy tone to disguise his sudden feeling of breathlessness. That had been his true intention, but it had been a mistake.

Basta!

She had a truly beautiful body, lush, ripe and tempting, when in his experience women tended to starve themselves into resembling stick insects in the name of fashion. Looking at the bountiful curves that almost seemed to be pleading to be freed of the unnatural constraint of confining white cotton was not enough. He wanted to touch.

He bunched his hands into fists at his side, his nails digging punishingly into the palms. If he could be aroused by a mercenary little tramp then he'd obviously been without a woman for far too long!

He bore the sounds of rustling fabric and little breathy grunts as long as he could before he bit out impatiently, 'Come. We are already late.' And he turned to meet a pair of anguished eyes peering through a curtain of tousled silky blonde hair.

She was hopping about on one foot, trying to fasten the buckle of a flat-soled sandal, her full mouth turned down at the corners as if she might burst into tears at any moment, and an incomprehensible wave of compassion surged through him.

In that strange, bunchy dress she looked like a waif. An appealing waif, he amended grudgingly, her throat so vulnerably slender as it rose from the oddly puckered collar, her feet so tiny in those practical, ugly plastic sandals. His lids felt strangely heavy, and his lashes lowered as he watched her plant both feet on the floor and tug at the belted waistline, as if trying to make the clumsily sewn hem hang more evenly.

'Satisfied?'

She'd hurled the question at him, and that was a confrontational tone if ever he'd heard one. Because he suddenly and inexplicably felt he knew just how awkward she must be feeling, he said with low-voiced gruff humour, 'You'll do. At least you're not inflicting the green frogs on my father.'

Her immediate answering smile made him blink. It was radiant. She had a cute little dimple at one corner of her mouth and those water-clear grey eyes sparkled with silver lights as she confirmed, 'They're something else, aren't they? Betty, my friend, gave them to me, so I had to wear them. It would have been unkind not to. But I would keep tripping over them—they are so huge!'

Lucenzo flattened his mouth as something dangerously akin to empathy flared inside him, then turned and strode to the door, holding it open. Was she really so ingenuous, or was it an act? The latter, most probably.

No woman who deliberately got pregnant by a wealthy married man and wielded the coming child like a weapon could possibly be guileless, he reminded himself. But, seeing the reluctant droop of her slight shoulders as she followed him through the door, he put his distrust of her on hold for the run-up to her first meeting with his father.

'I didn't intend this,' he admitted honestly. 'I

thought it best that you kept to your room and met my father in the morning. But he had other ideas and at the moment I'm humouring him when possible.'

Of course he was! Portia instantly forgave him for dragging her away from the safe cocoon of the nursery and Assunta's friendly, outgoing company. She straightened her shoulders. It was high time she stopped thinking of her own fears and miseries. 'Is he very ill?' she asked with soft sympathy.

Lucenzo turned, glancing down at her upturned face. She was right to care, he thought cynically. Eduardo Verdi was the only ally she had in this household.

'When he heard of Vittorio's death he suffered a stroke,' he offered, his mouth compressed. He ignored the shocked inward tug of her breath. 'Which was why he was unable to travel to England to attend the funeral. However, it was very slight and he will make a full recovery. In the meantime,' he warned grimly, 'my father is not to be upset or worried.'

As if she would do any such thing, Portia thought miserably, wishing with all her heart that Lucenzo didn't feel duty-bound to think the worst of her in every way there was.

Her eyes on the rich red carpet beneath her feet, she followed Lucenzo down a wide, door-lined corridor, trying to prepare herself mentally for the meeting ahead. But her mind kept flittering all over the place. She wondered if Assunta knew that if little Sam woke he'd go right back to sleep again if she turned him over, tucked him in and stroked his forehead for a few minutes, wondered how long dinner would last and whether the other, unknown, members of the family would treat her like an outcast.

They had passed the head of the main staircase what seemed like ages ago, and in a brave attempt to break the forbidding silence and lighten the atmosphere she said chirpily, 'If I'm let out of my room on my own I'm going to need a ball of string to find my way back again!'

Which was probably one of her more inappropriate remarks—the sort of thing she tended to blurt out without thinking, she decided sinkingly as Lucenzo clipped, 'I'm sure you'll quickly get used to it.' And that was on a par with the comment he'd made earlier about rushing to get her feet under the table, she decided, feeling well and truly quashed.

'For the moment my father is using a suite of rooms on the ground floor,' he explained chillingly.

They approached the head of another sweeping staircase and descended into a vast and echoey marble-paved hallway, then through an arched doorway and into a sombre room where a white-haired elderly man sat facing the door, his hands gripping the arms of his wheelchair as if he were in a state of acute anxiety.

Portia's heart melted immediately. The poor old gentleman was just as nervous about this meeting as she had been right up to this very moment!

Sparing only the briefest glance for the woman in what she took to be a nurse's uniform stationed behind the wheelchair, and hardly noticing Lucenzo's dry words of introduction, Portia sped over the dark, sumptuous carpet and took Eduardo's shakily out-stretched hand in both of hers.

'I'm so happy to meet you, and I'm so sorry you haven't been well,' she said warmly, inwardly an-guishing over the gaunt lines of his still handsome face, the brightness of what could be tears in the dark eyes that were so like Lucenzo's. The fingers that clasped her own seemed so very frail, Portia thought anxiously, swallowing around the emotional lump in her throat.

But there was nothing frail about Eduardo Verdi's voice as he said, albeit slowly, 'Welcome to Villa Fontebella, Portia. You have all you need? And my grandson? Is he settled?'

The bright, dark eyes narrowed as he attempted to penetrate the gloom of the room, as if he expected—hoped—to see the baby pop up from behind one or other of the shadowy pieces of furniture. Had he asked to see his grandson and Lucenzo had ruled it out of order? And why were the louvres almost closed over the many windows that marched down the length of the room? Wouldn't it be kinder to allow the old gen-tleman to see the sky, watch the shadows lengthen over the gardens?

'Sam's fast asleep,' she explained gently. 'It's been a long day for him. But I'll bring him to visit you in the morning, I promise. You'll love him; I know you will.' How could anyone not love the little darling? 'He's only two months old, but he's really alert and smiles at simply everyone! Meanwhile...'

She'd spied a tapestry-covered footstool and hooked

it towards her with one sandalled foot, settling down on it, hitching it closer to the wheelchair and delving in her handbag for her photographs. She'd taken simply loads with her instamatic and she pressed them into the waiting hands.

'Light!' Eduardo ordered imperiously, and Lucenzo stepped forward to position a standard lamp and switch it on.

He glanced at his watch. 'We don't have much time, Father, if you insist on joining the family for dinner. Perhaps you could look at them later, or in the morning.'

To Portia's secret delight Eduardo ignored him, and from the corner of her eye she watched the younger man retreat, his impressive features grim. A tiny shiver trickled down her spine. There was no doubt about who would have been giving the orders around here had his father not been ill and in need of humouring!

Turning, she gave her full attention to Eduardo, giving a running commentary as he eagerly sifted through the photographs depicting every stage of development in his grandson's short life. When he came to one of her favourites he commented, smiling, 'So many flowers! You must be a popular young lady!'

One of the hard-pressed nurses had obligingly taken it for her, and there she was, sitting in her hospital bed with a grin wide enough to crack her face, proudly holding the day-old Sam in her arms, surrounded by enough flowers to stock a florist's shop.

'People were so kind,' she murmured, smoothing a strand of silky blond hair behind one ear, settling in for a nice long chat. For the first time she was happy to be here, if only because looking at the pictures of his grandson gave the old gentleman so much pleasure.

'Do you see those roses?' They could hardly be missed; great bunches of them festooned the foot of the bed. 'Ethel Phipps, one of our neighbours, picked them for me. She must have denuded her garden. Wasn't that sweet of her? She paid the paper boy to bring them because she hardly ever gets out, poor old soul, on account of her arthritis.'

Her small face clouded momentarily. 'I hope she's all right. I do her weekly shop for her,' she explained earnestly. 'But I made Mum promise to look in on her while I'm away.'

'And your mother keeps her promises?'

'Always,' Portia acknowledged rapidly. 'She's a very moral person.' Then she turned bright pink, because Lucenzo was listening to every word and she knew he thought that, unlike her mother, she didn't have a moral worth mentioning.

But Eduardo soothed her ruffled feathers, handing back the photographs with a smile that was truly heartening, telling her, '*Ottimo!* Then you won't have to worry about your old lady while you are with us. That is good.' He lifted his head, still smiling. 'Come, Lucenzo. We go to dine.'

Lucenzo, lounging elegantly against the doorframe, a look of resignation on his darkly handsome face, moved forwards just as the nurse vented a flow of rapid and indignant-sounding Italian.

Portia gave her a startled glance. She'd forgotten the woman's presence—she'd been so wrapped up in showing Sam's photographs to his grandfather. She shuddered. The nurse looked alarming, as if she ate bricks for breakfast.

'My nurse is objecting,' Eduardo translated wryly. 'She is trying to insist that I eat here, alone, from a tray. As usual.' He dismissed the grim-faced woman with a formal nod of his silver head. 'I am ready, Lucenzo. Portia is about to meet the family—your aunt and your cousin, not forgetting Vito's widow— and we start as we mean to go on.'

Which sounded pretty disheartening to say the very least. Portia quailed. But she managed a weak smile and fell in beside Lucenzo as he carefully pushed the wheelchair through the double doors and down seemingly endless corridors. The prospect of meeting the rest of Vito's no doubt disapproving family and, horror of horrors, his poor grieving widow didn't exactly make her feel ecstatic.

But she'd weather it somehow. Her middle name wasn't Chickenheart, was it?

But it wasn't Braveheart, either!

CHAPTER FIVE

ACRES of gleaming mahogany, great swathes of silver and crystal—every piece glittering beneath the spectacular overhead chandelier, a different wine with each course and enough confusing cutlery to equip an army.

Throughout the seemingly interminable meal Portia had done her best to make herself smaller, wishing she were invisible. She had only managed to actually speak when directly, and always kindly, addressed by Signor Eduardo, merely dredging up a sickly, panicky smile when on the receiving end of an occasional barbed comment coming from Tia Donatella or her youthful son Giovanni.

The recently widowed Lorna hadn't spoken to her at all, not one word, and Portia really couldn't blame her. She wouldn't speak to her either, if she were in the other woman's shoes!

Now, pushing her spoon through some gooey sweet concoction, she despondently wished she'd never agreed to come here. Kind though Signor Eduardo was, it was an impossible situation—and, as if to highlight her position as a rank outsider and quite definitely *de trop*, both the other women were wearing the elegant, unrelieved black of mourning, while she stuck out like a sore thumb in her bunchy, cobbled together blue and cream thing.

68

And the way Giovanni looked at her made her feel even worse. His mouth might be turned down disapprovingly, but his sly eyes seemed to be mentally undressing her.

Lucenzo spoke at last, with a dip of his sleek head towards the footman—or whatever he called himself—who had been hovering throughout the meal, serving them from the endless dishes sent through from the kitchens, before turning to his parent, 'You are overtiring yourself, Father. Ugo will take you back to your room.'

Portia stumbled clumsily to her feet, nervous tension creating a tight band of pain across her forehead. Her mouth dry, she murmured to no one in particular, 'I'll say goodnight, too. Thank you, it was a lovely meal.'

Though she had barely swallowed a bite—course after course of mangled food having been whisked away from in front of her only to be replaced by something else to be mindlessly pushed around her plate.

And so she wallowed—she knew she was wallowing and her eyes blurred with shame and humiliation—in the wake of the only friend she had in this country, whom the footman, Ugo, was swiftly and efficiently wheeling away.

Until the grip of firm fingers on her arms halted her and Lucenzo said, 'Wait. You will see Father again in the morning. He's had enough excitement for one evening. I'll come for you and his grandson tomorrow at ten.'

Knowing he was right—of course he was right—

Portia wilted as his hands dropped back to his sides. She had so wanted to say a proper goodnight to Signor Eduardo, to round the dreadful evening off with just one kindly word. But that was simply selfish. The poor old gentleman deserved his rest, and already her arrival had forced him to introduce her to his sister, his nephew and his daughter-in-law, and endure the gruesome atmosphere at dinner.

Her head bowed with misery, she turned to retrace her steps and blundered into an ornate side table which held a silver epergne full of fragrant blossoms. Automatically she apologised. Though why she should say sorry to a table and a bunch of flowers she had no idea. She giggled hysterically to herself at the very moment her eyes filled with emotional tears.

'Are you drunk?'

Lucenzo tersely scanned her face. She was swaying on her feet, as if she could barely stand, and looked as if she couldn't decide whether to laugh or whether to cry and so had compromised by doing both at once.

And she sounded far from sober as she wailed back at him, 'No, I am not drunk!'

'You ate next to nothing. I watched. And the wine was flowing.'

If she stayed here long enough he would get round to accusing her of every crime in the book! A stab of sheer rage hit Portia somewhere in the region of her ribcage. She pulled in a very deep breath and shot him an angry glance.

'If you were watching that closely you'd have known I only drank one mouthful. I don't like the taste. I prefer cider. Sweet cider,' she added with an attempt at haughtiness that brought a gleam to his eyes and a twitch to his long, sensual mouth. Her small chin lifted stubbornly. 'I'm tired, that's all. And I want to check on Sam.'

'Then I'll see you to your rooms.'

'There's no need.' Portia rubbed her eyes wearily. The spurt of anger had fired her up but the effects had worn off all too quickly, leaving her feeling even more drained than she had before.

But after the frightfulness of dinner with the family she didn't have enough energy left to argue when Lucenzo cupped her elbow with one firm hand, and could only raise the palest ghost of a smile as he steered her down the hushed, softly lit corridor and commented drily, 'There's every need. You forgot your ball of string.'

The warmth of his hand was comforting, she reluctantly admitted, his mere physical presence a kind of solace. And she was too weary and dispirited to try to find excuses for such a lame and spineless admission.

The weak temptation to lean against him seemed to pervade every pore of her body, but she gritted her teeth and resisted it. She was a responsible, adult woman, wasn't she? She didn't need to lean on anyone! And she had her child to think of.

At the thought of Sam her pace quickened. What if he had missed her, had been crying his little heart out while she'd been wallowing in her own selfish misery? Her heart was beating like a drum, guilt making her feel almost physically sick as Lucenzo at last opened the door to the suite of rooms she'd been given.

Silence. A brief moment of deep relief, then the blood-freezing thought that her darling baby might have smothered himself in his sleep. She roughly jerked her arm from Lucenzo's grasp just as Assunta emerged from the sitting room Portia hadn't even poked her nose in yet.

'I thought I heard you.' The Italian woman beamed. 'The little one has been fed and changed and sleeps peacefully again. I will come in the morning, about eight—unless you need anything more this evening?'

'I—Oh, no, of course not.' Portia floundered. Assunta was carrying a tray of empty dishes. The poor woman had had to eat up here, alone, she thought remorsefully. She really shouldn't have left her babysitting for so long. 'I'm really sorry I've been so long,' she apologised contritely.

She should have been strong-minded enough to tell Signor Eduardo that, no offence intended, but she wouldn't share dinner with the family this evening. Her place was with her baby. Hadn't her mother often complained that her puppy-dog eagerness to please others was one of the worst of her myriad failings?

'Don't be silly!' Assunta chided comfortably. 'Helping you with the little one is my job from now on. Besides, nothing could give me greater pleasure.'

The remark was meant to be reassuring; Portia knew that. But it didn't, somehow, hit the spot. Assunta was a nice lady, but she was very determined, too. Was she part of some hidden agenda? A plot to separate her from her baby eventually?

The knot that had been growing deep inside her stomach suddenly tightened and, leaving Lucenzo saying something to his former nanny, Portia sped into the nursery. By the dim night-light she devoured Sam's tiny face, the way his little arms were flung above his head, until the knot untied itself and she was breathing more normally.

She would do better in future, she vowed silently. She wouldn't let herself be pushed around. It had been a mistake to come here, but the damage wasn't permanent.

In a few days' time she would gently but firmly tell Sam's grandfather that she could only stay here for a week or two. Explain that she had every intention of bringing his grandson back for visits, and that when he himself was fully fit again he could come and stay with them in England whenever he wanted, for as long as he wanted. Though quite how she would square that with her parents, or find the money for flights to and from Tuscany, she had no idea.

'Satisfied?' Lucenzo's soft voice behind her made her leap out of her skin. She had believed him to be long gone. Her hand flew to her throat to still the frantic pulse-beat and he commented drily, 'As you see, he hasn't been spirited away while your back was turned or been force-fed with steak and kidney pudding. Assunta will always take great care of him.'

'I'm sure she will. When I need her to, that is.' Her reply was stiff and she couldn't respond to his brand of dry humour. She didn't like the sound of that 'always' bit at all. Casting one last loving look at her peacefully sleeping son, she turned and left the room, waiting until Lucenzo joined her before quietly pulling the nursery door to, leaving it a little ajar the better to hear Sam when he woke in the night.

Alone with him now in the warm, dimly lit silence of her bedroom, Portia felt her heart begin to race. The height of him, the breadth of him suddenly seemed to overwhelm her. She could feel the tension, sharp and insistent, and shivered with reaction. He was watching her, his eyes a darkly veiled hypnotic glitter reaching deep inside her soul, making her feel a wild yearning for something only dimly guessed at. She knew she had to make him go before she said or did something that would make the humiliation of this evening worse—something she would regret for perhaps the rest of her life.

Dragging her eyes from his, she stared at her feet, at the practical but ugly sandals she'd bought in a closing-down sale. There was danger in the way she felt so drawn to him, like a moth to a flame, a kind of madness because she knew exactly what he thought of her. Her voice came out thickly, almost on a whisper. 'Please go.'

'Of course. When you've eaten.'

'I've already—'

'No, you haven't. I was watching you, remember?'

Portia lifted uncomprehending eyes and met the blankness of his. She shuddered as he moved, placed a hand on the small of her back and propelled her over the soft carpet towards the open door to the sitting room. There, strategically placed table lamps cast a warm and welcoming glow over exquisitely upholstered armchairs, a pretty writing desk and low tables, one bearing a bowl of flowers which perfumed the air, another with a tray.

'I asked Assunta to send Paolina up with a light supper,' he explained. 'If you don't eat you won't sleep, and you look exhausted.'

He lifted a silver cover to reveal a steaming omelette. There was a bowl of green salad too, she noted, another of diced fresh fruit, a glass of creamy milk.

'Thank you. That was thoughtful.' It was an effort to get the words out, but her heart warmed a little. She really hadn't expected much in the way of kindness from him. Knowing what he thought of her, it was completely unexpected and, oddly, made her want to cry.

She wasn't hungry, though. The mere thought of eating made her stomach churn, and she wondered frantically how she could dispose of the food without being found out, because she didn't want to hurt the feelings of whoever had gone to the trouble of preparing the tray for her.

Twisting her hands together she said, 'Goodnight,' in what she hoped was a tone of polite but firm dismissal.

But Lucenzo gave her a small humourless smile and stated, 'I'll go when you've eaten. Every scrap.'

He meant every word of it; she could see that, she thought morosely. With a sigh of sheer fatalism she perched on the extreme edge of an armchair, tugged the tray towards her over the shiny surface of the low table, gave him a thin smile and grumbled, 'You're just like my mother!'

As Lucenzo took the chair that was angled towards hers he murmured drily, 'You liken me, Lucenzo Verdi, to a middle-aged lady?' and for Portia the atmosphere lightened, just a little.

He hadn't taken offence, despite his words. There was a gleam of humour in his fine eyes, and a barely controlled twitch played around his beautiful mouth. She felt the weight of his constant displeasure lift from her weary shoulders, and that led her to pick up a fork and dig it into the omelette she hadn't wanted.

It was light and fluffy and stuffed with buttery mushrooms—and quite, quite delicious. She explained earnestly through a mouthful, 'I didn't mean you look like a sixty-year-old retired schoolmistress—you just have the same attitude. Domineering, cold, always telling me what to do.'

'I am not always cold,' he replied softly, and Portia shot him a startled look. Relaxed back in the chair, his long legs outstretched, he was watching her from beneath lowered lids, and something in those veiled eyes sent a fizzy shiver down her spine.

Smartly averting her eyes, she reapplied herself to the last of the omelette. But her throat felt tight and it was difficult to swallow, and her body jerked involuntarily as he asked, 'Did you always do as you were told?'

He saw her rigid shoulders relax as she responded

to the lightness of his tone, and the compassion he'd felt over the last couple of hours became more securely grounded. Dinner had been a desperate ordeal for her, in spite of his father's attempts to put her at her ease, and against all of his instincts he'd pitied her deeply when she'd clumsily blundered away from the table in Ugo's wheelchair-pushing wake.

When he'd prevented her from following she'd seemed so disorientated, utterly exhausted, and all he'd done, he reminded himself sourly, was to accuse her of being drunk!

Despite what he knew of her lack of morals, you couldn't help feeling sorry for another human being who was floundering way out of their depth. 'So,' he prompted gently, 'did you always follow orders?'

He watched a sad little smile wipe some of the weariness from her face as she laid down her fork and turned to him.

'I did try, really hard, but I couldn't live up to their expectations,' she explained mournfully as the thick sweep of her lashes lowered over her clear grey gaze. 'You see, they were both school teachers, academics and set in their ways. They married quite late and I came as something of a surprise, but once I arrived on the scene they sort of hatched all these ambitious plans for me. Barrister, surgeon, mathematician—there were loads of options, or so they were always telling me. They expected me to be clever. But I wasn't. I was just a great big disappointment.'

And they made good and sure she knew it, he

thought on a stir of resentment. Poor kid. Was that why she often looked so unsure of herself?

'And what about you? What did you want?' he asked gruffly, and she lifted her eyes and smiled at him. A real smile this time, lighting up the whole of her face, making her look almost beautiful. Her teeth were even, pearly white, her full lips glistening, and he wondered if she would taste of butter if he kissed her.

Fool! He caught the thought and kicked it out of play, shifting uncomfortably, and heard her say on a lilt of rueful amusement, 'They wanted me to have some high-powered career or other, and all I ever wanted was my own home, children—the whole domestic bit.'

A gear shifted in Lucenzo's brain. He leant forward, his hands on his knees, his black eyes intense. Because she had wanted a child had she lied to Vito, told him she was protected? Had she been desperate to conceive a baby—by any man? Had he misjudged her in that?

Had the financial support of a seriously wealthy family ever entered the equation? Judging by her obvious uneasiness at the ostentatious display of wealth at dinner tonight, the way she'd seemed afraid to touch the Venetian glass, the heavy silver, the delicate china, perhaps not.

'Was that why you slept with Vittorio? Because you wanted a child?'

Portia's mouth fell open and she looked at him blankly, for all the world as if he'd spoken in Swahili, before she blurted hotly, 'No! Of course not! I made *love*,' she stressed vehemently, 'because poor Vito wanted to so badly.'

Out of duty, really, she recognised as soon as she'd finished speaking, and the shock of hindsight made her soft mouth tremble. Vito had been begging and begging her, telling her he wanted her so much he couldn't concentrate on the work that was so vital to their future. In the end she'd given in, on the face of it to celebrate their unofficial engagement, relegating her possibly strait-laced intention of waiting until their wedding night to the back burner. A wedding night that would never have come, she now knew, of course.

Feeling faintly ridiculous, and not a little resentful at the way Lucenzo was prying into her private life, she bit down on her lower lip and glared at him through the long sweep of her lashes. And then she stopped breathing. His eyes were impossibly magnetic in his lean, handsome face; she couldn't have looked away to save her life. All sorts of strange sensations were chasing each other up and down her spine, pooling in a starburst of excitement deep inside her.

One black brow rose just slightly, his mouth curved softly, and his voice was a wicked murmur as he asked, 'Are you always so generous, Portia? If I said I wanted you would you sleep with me?'

CHAPTER SIX

WHY couldn't she get it out of her mind? Portia asked herself distractedly, her mind in a wild tangle. She was trying her hardest to concentrate on the look of deep pleasure on Eduardo's lined face as he held the burbling Sam on his knee, but she couldn't stop thinking of the question Lucenzo had asked in that low, awesomely sexy voice of his: 'If I said I wanted you would you sleep with me?'

She'd gone to pieces inside, everything fizzing and melting, breathless and quivering, her mouth dry, pulses skittering all over the place as she'd imagined what it would be like to make love with him. And she'd tried to hide it, tried so desperately that she'd been rigid with the effort as she'd got to her feet and flung, 'Get out!' right in his devastatingly attractive face.

It hadn't been a pass; of course it hadn't. Lucenzo wouldn't make a pass at the likes of her; she just knew he wouldn't. He'd simply been rubbing in the utterly humiliating fact that he thought she was anybody's. But even knowing that hadn't stopped her wretched body going into bedroom mode!

It was simply awful! She didn't understand herself. She'd truly believed she was in love with Vito, but going to bed with him hadn't sparked any kind of conflagration inside her. The only pleasure she'd had, had come from knowing she'd made him happy.

She rubbed her damp palms down the sides of her jeans and shuffled her bottom on the seat of her chair. Everything would be a darn sight easier if Lucenzo weren't here, leaning against one of the tall window frames and watching proceedings from those dangerously enigmatic lowered eyes of his.

As they'd been last evening, the louvres were almost closed, filtering out the daylight, but thankfully the grim-faced, super-starched nurse had gone on her coffee break, leaving Lucenzo in charge to see that she and Sam didn't bore or overtire his father.

Not that the old gentleman seemed to be either, she noted, watching his face light up as his newly introduced little grandson blew gurgling bubbles at him. If only Lucenzo would make himself scarce then she wouldn't feel like an insect on a pin. Or feel the unwelcome tingle of awareness that now was par for the course whenever he was around. Or have face-ache from wearing a forced and often faltering smile which had to be very firmly twitched back into place every time it slipped.

'He has the look of his father,' Eduardo Verdi pronounced with evident satisfaction, just as a chirping sound broke into the quietness.

Lucenzo fished a slender mobile phone from the back pocket of his dark grey trousers, made a few light responses, then thrust it back where it had come from.

A few rapid words in Italian to his father, and to

Portia, tonelessly, 'I have to go. Please stay until the nurse returns.'

She watched him stride from the room with a peculiar mixture of relief and loss—glad to see him leave, yet desperately wanting him to stay—and wondered if the awful situation she found herself in was making her lose what little brainpower she did have.

'Shall I take him, Signor Verdi, if he's tiring you?' she asked, determined to do her very best to concentrate on poor Vito's sick father and put her own troubles firmly to the back of her mind.

'He's not tiring me in the least. He is my grandson! And please, Portia, less of the Signor Verdi. I would prefer it if you would use my given name.' He gave her a level, kindly look. 'You and I have much to say to each other. But first—' his dark eyes gleamed mischievously '—do you think you could let a little light into this room, while my jailor's away? I object to living in such gloom.'

'Of course!' Portia sprang to her feet, her spirits lifting. Eduardo's views coincided exactly with her own. The battle-axe nurse must have decreed that the poor old gentleman lived in semi-darkness, and that couldn't be good for anyone.

As she turned from flooding the room with welcome full daylight she noted that Eduardo didn't look sick at all. He actually looked quite perky, and younger than she'd imagined him to be when they'd met last evening. In his late fifties, maybe?

Emboldened by his smile of approval, she slid open the glass doors that led directly onto the terrace and breathed in the warm air, the scent of a myriad blossoms.

'I'm not a trained medic,' she confided with a broad smile that made her face incandescent, 'but I'm sure fresh air and sunlight can't do any harm.'

'Just what I've been telling that wretched woman Lucenzo insisted on hiring!' he agreed vehemently. 'Her ideas are as outdated as the dodo. And don't think I haven't tried to get rid of her—I have. But, so she informs me, she takes her orders only from Lucenzo!'

'I expect he thinks he's doing what's best for you,' Portia soothed, sympathising with every word he said but not wanting to see him getting too agitated. 'I'll have a word with him. I know I'd get depressed if I were shut away in a darkened room! I'm sure you'd benefit from a little stimulation, too—a few gentle outings. I'll tell him so.'

And so she would. She might be easy-going, but she could get quite fierce over things she felt strongly about. Though getting Lucenzo to agree with her opinions might be uphill work.

'And talking of outings—' she gestured impulsively to the open glass doors '—shall we?'

'Why not?'

His delighted grin, the way he shouted for joy when he managed to release the brake, confirmed Portia's opinion that she was doing the right thing. She pushed the wheelchair to the far end of the long terrace, parking it beneath the dappled shade of a canopy of vines, perching herself on the stone balustrading right next to him so that she could keep her eyes on her baby, who was expressing his delight in the outing by vigorously waving his arms and legs in the air. Like a fat little beetle on its back, she thought fondly.

'You have a beautiful home,' she said appreciatively, 'and I've never seen anything to touch these gardens. You know something? If someone could construct a temporary ramp over those steps for your chair we could take a stroll each morning before it gets too hot, all three of us.'

'Bless you!' His voice sounded rough round the edges and his dark eyes were suddenly suspiciously bright. 'Portia, my dear, I swear you're better than any tonic! A ramp for the terrace steps sounds like a splendid idea—but I warn you, I'll be on my feet in no time and taking this little fellow fishing as soon as he can walk! And as for my family home—it's your home now.'

Which sounded as though he believed their stay here would be permanent, Portia thought sinkingly. How could she tell him that it wasn't, that she'd be taking his grandson back to England? Tell him she must, of course. But later, when she was sure he was stronger.

Sam was getting restless now, and, glad of the distraction, Portia swallowed the lump in her throat and took him from Eduardo's arms, holding him over her shoulder, patting his back, rocking him.

He was due for a feed, but Lucenzo had told her to stay with his father until the nurse reappeared and she could hardly leave Eduardo on his own. So it was with some relief when she saw Assunta appear through the sliding doors. She could grandpa-sit!

'What a happy picture you all make! I'm glad to see you enjoying the air, *signor*. I will take the little one. It is time.'

With a pang, Portia relinquished her tiny son. But he'd be fine with Assunta, she knew that, and wondered if she'd always feel this possessive, as if she couldn't bear to be parted from him, even for a second.

'Assunta will take every care of him,' Eduardo said gently, as if he knew exactly what she was feeling. 'She was a young girl when she came to us and has been with us ever since. She looked after Lucenzo almost from the first—Vittorio, too. I think she was both mother and father to them. I, alas, didn't see as much of either of them as I should have done.

'Apart from burying myself in my work at the bank, Lucenzo was away at school and, as I expect Vito told you, his mother and I parted ways when he was young. I made the mistake of allowing her to take him back to her homeland—your country. Naturally, he made regular visits throughout his growing years, but it wasn't the same. I should never have allowed her to have custody. I could easily have stopped it. A son is a son, after all. Important.'

Would he place the same importance on a grandson? Portia thought with a plummeting heart. Would the united power of the Verdi family come into play when she announced her intention to take her son back to England, dragging her endlessly through the courts, as Lucenzo had threatened they would?

'But enough of that.' Eduardo regarded her smilingly before his mouth straightened. 'I want to apologise for the way my family behaved at dinner last night. They are good-hearted people, but once they get an idea in their heads it gets stuck there. When I heard of your existence, that you'd given birth to Vittorio's child, I had no such preconceptions. I wanted to meet you before I made up my mind as to your motivations and character. Just one look at you, a few minutes' conversation, and anyone with a grain of sense would know you weren't a scheming minx with her eye on the main chance! Give them time and they'll come to their senses—or have me to answer to! I may be confined to this chair at the moment but I am still head of this family!'

'Oh, please—' Portia was appalled. 'I don't want to be the cause of any bad feelings. It doesn't matter; it really doesn't,' she objected miserably.

'It matters,' Eduardo asserted stoutly, and then, more softly, 'You have nothing to be ashamed of. Vito must have loved you deeply. You and he would have been married as soon as his divorce came through—it is what he would have intended. I know—knew—my son.'

His voice faltered briefly and Portia felt her heart clench with sympathy, admiring the strength of his character when he cleared his throat and continued firmly, 'I knew he wasn't remotely in love with his wife, and Lorna certainly wasn't in love with him. It was fairly common knowledge. That marriage was unsatisfactory right from the start. But what can one do?

Or say? You can't live your children's lives for them. You have to let them make their own mistakes and hope they learn from them.'

Portia swallowed jerkily. This was awful—almost as bad as the way Lucenzo viewed her: with suspicion and contempt. Like Assunta, Eduardo was seeing her affair with Vito as high romance; they didn't know he had lied to her, deceived her in the cruellest way possible.

She certainly couldn't shatter their illusions, which meant that her presence here was shoring up a lie. She vented a silent sigh, and was almost glad to see the hatchet face of Eduardo's nurse as she stamped towards them and wheeled her resigned charge away with a volley of staccato Italian grumblings.

Portia was very afraid she'd got Eduardo into big trouble. She should have thought things through, she decided guiltily, biting her lip, asked before she took matters into her own hands in her usual reckless fashion.

Unable to face watching Assunta feed and change little Sam while her own state of mind was in such wretched turmoil, she walked down the steps from the terrace between banks of perfumed roses. The sky was a perfect blue, the sun growing hotter and the gardens were silent apart from the sound of her feet on the narrow gravel paths that bordered the formal beds.

She had the place to herself and that helped to calm her, just a little. Lucenzo had disappeared, poor Eduardo would be shut away in that gloomy room, and the others would probably be getting ready for lunch—drinking cocktails or whatever the super-rich did to pass the morning. Whatever happened, she would not be joining them. She had enough to think about without having to squirm beneath more of their cold contempt.

Coming across a stone fountain in the centre of the paved square from which all the narrow paths radiated, she held a hand beneath the cool tumbling water, breathed in deeply and released the pent-up air on a long sigh.

And jumped two feet in the air when a lean, lightly tanned hand clamped down on her shoulder and Lucenzo said drily, 'Sighing for your sins?'

The pressure of his fingers increased as he swung her round to face him, and a sensation of hot breathlessness swamped her, making any kind of response impossible. In the sunlight his dark eyes glinted with mesmerising silver lights, holding her immobile. She just stared at him, unable to look away, her throat going hot and dry.

She swallowed hard and flicked her tongue over her arid lips, forcing herself to say something, anything, just so he wouldn't know how strangely he affected her.

'You made me jump.'

'So I saw. Guilty conscience?' he asked impassively, then coolly elaborated in the dry drawl that made every inch of her skin prickle and burn. 'I've come from speaking with my father and receiving a catalogue of complaints from his nurse.'

'Oh, goodness!' Portia's face went pale. 'You

mustn't blame him; it was all my fault,' she mumbled guiltily, looking at the ground and wishing it would swallow her up. 'I suggested we went outside. Is he all right? You haven't upset him, have you?'

Lucenzo's mouth curved as he regarded the top of her downbent head. 'He's fine. He's with his physiotherapist at the moment and looking brighter and happier than I've seen him since we heard of Vittorio's accident.'

The shoulders that had been hunched up around Portia's neck slowly relaxed. At least it didn't sound as if she'd earned Eduardo a lecture. He wouldn't be looking bright and happy if she had.

The 'catalogue of complaints' must have been directed at her, which was fair enough. She lifted her head and fixed her eyes on his. 'I'm not going to apologise for taking your father out onto the terrace—' she stated firmly.

'No one's asking you to.' The firm mouth quirked. 'Except, perhaps, his nurse. And she's been gently put in her place. From now on, until he's back on his feet, he's to have a good dose of fresh air and sunshine. Every morning. And in your company—yours and Sam's.'

It was the first time he'd called her baby by his given name. Up until now he'd referred to him as Vittorio's child, almost in denial of her own existence as the baby's mother. So did that mean he was growing to accept her?

Her heart swelled with pleasure at the mere thought, but when she felt the colour rush back into her face she told herself not to be so darn stupid. She flicked her eyes away from him and turned round to face the fountain, blocking him out because he was looking at her with such a strange intensity it made all her bones go weak.

Lucenzo fought back the urge to manhandle her, to force her to face him again so that he could see every nuance of expression on her face, find the elusive truth.

His father thought she ought to be wearing a halo, had said she was the best thing to happen to him in longer than he could remember. But that could have a lot to do with holding his first grandchild, the unexpected freedom of an hour in the open air. Which, he admitted heavily, was partly his own fault.

He'd been so intent on following the regime the hired nurse had prescribed to the letter, believing she knew best, he hadn't looked at things from the invalid's viewpoint. Vittorio's woman had. For one reason or another.

He recalled the way she'd been at her first meeting with his father, the completely natural way she'd broken the ice between them, sitting at his feet, fishing those photographs out of her handbag, chattering nineteen to the dozen as if they'd known each other for years.

Why? Because she had a schemer's natural instinct and ability to wheedle her way into her target's affections? Or was what you saw what you got? A naive innocent whose only ambition was to be everybody's best friend?

He said, perhaps more brusquely than he'd intended, 'You've made a good impression on my father. I value him; we all do. So, whatever your reasons, be sure you keep it up. I won't see him disillusioned or hurt.'

Portia roughly swallowed around the thick lump that had immediately risen in her throat. So much for him growing to accept her—that 'whatever your reasons' said it all, didn't it just? He was light years away from trusting her, let alone accepting her into his exalted family.

And then he added, 'That phone call was to let me know Nonna is ready to be collected. She's looking forward to meeting you at lunch and visiting the nursery to see Vittorio's child.'

Her stomach turned right over, making her feel quite ill. She did not want to have lunch with the Verdi family, or meet this Nonna person, whoever she might be, and endure another dose of hostile scrutiny—and Sam was back to being 'Vittorio's child'!

When she could trust herself to speak she turned, and, lower lip trembling, said what had to be said, 'I can't stay here.'

'Repeat that,' he ordered after a beat of total silence, his voice cold and cutting, his face a grim mask. To Portia he looked horribly threatening, not at all prepared to listen to reason.

Inwardly quailing, she nevertheless set her chin at a challenging angle. 'You heard! I'll stay for a couple of weeks—just for your father's sake. And I'll make it right with him before I take Sam back to England; I swear I will.'

Lucenzo stiffened. What game was she playing now? She'd already twisted his father round her little finger; she could live here in luxury, with servants to cater to her every whim. What more did she want?

His eyes narrowed as he bit out, 'I've already warned you of what will happen if you threaten to remove the child. You knew that before you arrived here. You are here because my father wanted it, not by my wish.' Grim eyes bored into her skull, as if he were trying to get into her mind. 'But now you are here you will stay. If you've got demands to make then make them now, but I warn you, I will not give in easily to blackmail.'

Portia's eyes widened in horror. Did he really think she was going to demand payment before she'd agree to stay on? She gave a mortified groan and whispered wretchedly, 'I'm not trying to blackmail anyone! You must see this is all a dreadful mistake! My being here at all must put an awful strain on your family. They're grieving for Vito and I don't want to add to their distress—and just think what it must be like for Vito's poor widow, having to see me and his child!'

Tears were falling now and she couldn't see him properly. His outline was blurry, receding and then looming closer. She scrubbed her eyes angrily, wanting to be calm and sensible but knowing she was losing it as all her mental turmoil surged to the surface, bubbling over.

'Eduardo thinks—he thinks Vito loved me, and

would have married me when—when he and Lorna parted,' she wailed unsteadily. 'How could I tell him the truth? It's—kinder to let him keep his illusions, isn't it? And as for the rest of you—looking down your superior noses at me and thinking I'm out for all I can get—well, I guess even you have hearts that are hurting over Vito's death, so why should I be here, making it harder? It's an impossible situation for all concerned.'

Portia put shaky fingers to her eyes to swipe the wretched tears away, deeply irritated with herself, wishing she could control her emotions. Or, better still, not have any!

He *had* moved closer. It hadn't just been the effects of her distorted vision. Too close. Her drenched eyes connected with Lucenzo's shimmering lancet gaze and held. He could make what he liked of what she'd said, argue until he was blue in the face and make his vile threats. She wouldn't change her mind.

Her outburst had been unexpected. It had shaken him. Either her distress was genuine or she was a truly brilliant actress. A slight frown line appeared between his eyes, deepening as he asked, 'What is the truth about your relationship with my brother?'

Scorn lifted her chin a fraction higher, narrowed her eyes. So now he was asking? Because she'd called his bluff and stated her intention of leaving? Never once had he expressed an interest in her side of the sorry story. He had just decided in that intimidating, arrogant way of his that she'd got pregnant on purpose, was out for all she could get from his family.

'You don't want to know!' she replied as haughtily as she could. 'It might put a stain on your precious family escutcheon!' Then she spoiled the effect by giving a noisy sniff and scrubbing at her face, where the hot sun had dried all those tears to itchy rivulets.

'Here—' His long mouth twitched as he reached in a back pocket for a pristine handkerchief, shaking out the folds before handing it to her. 'Blow your nose properly,' he ordered mildly—as if he were talking to a small grubby child, she thought on a stab of sharp annoyance as she did as she was told.

He, of course, was as immaculate as ever, she noted on a surge of spiky resentment. Not a dark hair out of place, his cool pale grey collarless silk shirt and toning chinos almost painfully elegant, while she was a hot sweaty mess, her cheap T-shirt sticking to her body and her workaday jeans a complete stranger to any-thing approaching a designer label.

'So tell me,' he urged quietly as she stuffed the handkerchief in a side pocket of her jeans. Her soft mouth, mutinously pouting, looked oddly appealing and he wondered, not for the first time, what it would taste like.

Impatience with himself for giving headroom to that line of thought unconsciously sharpened the edges of his voice, 'Lunch looms and Nonna is anxious to meet you. We don't have much time. Tell me what you think would upset my father. Or do I have to drag it from you?'

Troubled grey eyes met the dark incisiveness of his and her thick lashes fluttered. She didn't want to say hurtful things about his dead brother but he certainly did look as if he would drag the truth from her if he had to. Shakily, she said, 'You won't like it, and you probably won't believe it, but I never dreamed Vito was already married.'

He let that pass for the moment, asking, 'How did you meet?'

How cold his voice. In spite of the heat, Portia shivered.

'In the café where I worked. He'd been sitting there for a good hour. He looked really fed-up.' She gave a tiny sigh, a shrug of her neat-boned shoulders. 'He was at one of Betty's tables, and she'd already had a word with him—Mr Weston, the owner, didn't like it when customers sat over just one cup of coffee for ages.'

Betty had said, 'Quick, you go and talk to him, find out what's wrong. He looks as miserable as sin. Besides, he's too gorgeous to be tossed out into the street in this rain. I've already told him you're a pushover when it comes to people with problems! Take him another coffee before the boss asks him to leave.'

Remembering how it had all started made Portia feel so miserable, and duped. Her voice wobbly, she said out loud, 'I did go and talk to him. He said he'd been on his way back to London when his car had broken down. He'd phoned a friend who was coming to pick him up.'

If she hadn't talked to him, tried to cheer him up for half an hour, until her stint had ended, then none of this would have happened. But she couldn't really regret it, because if she hadn't met Vito then Sam wouldn't have been born and her baby was the most wonderful thing in her life.

'I never thought I'd see him again, but he turned up a week later, just as I was getting ready to leave. He insisted on taking me for supper—just a bar snack in the pub over the road—as a sort of thank you for getting him out of the doldrums when his old banger had died on him.'

Noting the way her hands were clasped so tightly in front of her, displaying her inner agitation, Lucenzo felt a knot of something beyond his powers of description tighten inside him. Some 'old banger'! He recalled his brother's fury and disgust when he'd recounted the way the latest sports car he'd paid a small fortune for had broken down on its first outing.

'And?' he prompted heavily. 'You went to bed with him?'

'No!' Her denial was immediate, horrified. 'We just talked. He told me all about himself. Said he was half-Italian, that he was working in a restaurant in London but he wanted to open his own in the town where I lived. That was why he visited now and then—to look for a suitable affordable property. And, well,' she confessed uncomfortably, 'we met up whenever he was in the area. I really liked him, and admired the way he was working so hard to make something of himself. And he said he loved me, that we'd be married when he had a place of his own. We even got engaged—'

She lifted doleful eyes to him, not expecting him to believe a word of what she was saying because he wouldn't want to think badly of Vito, who was no

The Harlequin Reader Service® — Here's how it works:

Accepting your 2 free books and gift places you under no obligation to buy anything. You may keep the books and gift and return the shipping statement marked "cancel." If you do not cancel, about a month later we'll send you 6 additional books and bill you just $3.57 each in the U.S., or $4.24 each in Canada, plus 25¢ shipping & handling per book and applicable taxes if any.* That's the complete price and — compared to cover prices of $4.25 each in the U.S. and $4.99 each in Canada — it's quite a bargain! You may cancel at any time, but if you choose to continue, every month we'll send you 6 more books, which you may either purchase at the discount price or return to us and cancel your subscription.

*Terms and prices subject to change without notice. Sales tax applicable in N.Y. Canadian residents will be charged applicable provincial taxes and GST.

If offer card is missing write to: The Harlequin Reader Service, 3010 Walden Ave., P.O. Box 1867, Buffalo, NY 14240-1867

NO POSTAGE
NECESSARY
IF MAILED
IN THE
UNITED STATES

BUSINESS REPLY MAIL

FIRST-CLASS MAIL   PERMIT NO. 717-003   BUFFALO, NY

POSTAGE WILL BE PAID BY ADDRESSEE

HARLEQUIN READER SERVICE
3010 WALDEN AVE
PO BOX 1867
BUFFALO NY 14240-9952

Do You Have the LUCKY KEY?

PLAY THE Lucky Key Game
and you can get

Scratch the gold areas with a coin. Then check below to see the books and gift you can get!

FREE BOOKS and a FREE GIFT!

YES! I have scratched off the gold areas. Please send me the 2 FREE BOOKS and GIFT for which I qualify. I understand I am under no obligation to purchase any books, as explained on the back of this card.

306 HDL DNVX   106 HDL DNVM

FIRST NAME	LAST NAME

ADDRESS

APT.#	CITY

STATE/PROV.	ZIP/POSTAL CODE

2 free books plus a free gift

2 free books

1 free book

Try Again!

Offer limited to one per household and not valid to current Harlequin Presents® subscribers. All orders subject to approval.

Visit us online at www.eHarlequin.com

DETACH AND MAIL CARD TODAY!

(H-P-07/02)

longer here to defend himself. 'I wouldn't let him spend any of his savings on a ring, but I did agree to spend a night with him.' Her face turned scarlet. 'He said it would seal our betrothal, that wanting me so much and not having me was burning him up,' she explained wretchedly. 'I swear I didn't know he was married. I knew nothing about who he really was until I saw the report of his accident in the morning paper.'

Lucenzo tugged in a harsh breath. Tears were glittering in her eyes again and her soft mouth was trembling. Everything she'd said rang true. Suddenly, without reservations, he believed her.

He knew exactly what his half-brother had been like and could see why he'd been attracted to her. She was all soft, womanly curves, her eyes were beautiful and when she smiled she was utterly lovely. She would have been a challenge his womanising half-brother would have been constitutionally unable to resist.

She was light years away from his usual bits on the side. Naive, soft-hearted, eager to please. But, in old-fashioned phraseology, she was a good girl—and that would have made the challenge more exciting. A fancy dinner, a ride in a flashy car, a bucket of champagne and a gift of jewellery wouldn't have got her into his bed.

It had taken a lot more effort. A line in sympathy-seeking, a load of lies and happy-ever-promises he'd had no intention of keeping.

His own attitude towards her hadn't helped the poor scrap. He'd given her a mountain of aggro. Learning the truth about Vittorio, in the most shocking way possible, must have shattered her. Yet, heavily pregnant with the child his half-brother would have surely disowned had he lived, she'd attended his funeral. Because she'd felt it her duty to pay her last respects to the father of her unborn child? It would have taken a great deal of courage.

And he hated to see her cry. A tide of sympathy, of self-disgust for the way he'd given her such a rough ride, blocked the air in his lungs. Expelling it slowly, he reached out his hands and cupped her face, hating the distress he saw in the wide grey eyes.

'Don't cry, Portia,' he murmured unevenly. And kissed her.

CHAPTER SEVEN

IT WAS like being swept into paradise, and Portia gasped inwardly as a wave of something too sublime to be recognised engulfed her.

The tingling ribbons of delicious shock that had invaded her entire nervous system when his mouth had first closed over hers were taking ages to die down, making her feel light-headed, incapable of moving, of doing a single thing except simply stand there, drowning in liquid fire, drawing raggedy little breaths as his fingers twined slowly through her hair, his lips moulding the contours of hers.

Every thought was blanked out, all her senses were wholly seduced, fiercely concentrated on the way his mouth felt against hers—just that. The way his lips were gently parting hers, the tip of his tongue moving languorously inside. And she was simply letting it happen, because it was so utterly and completely wonderful.

The first sign that he might be breaking the kiss, withdrawing this irresistible magic, made her give a throatily protesting moan, made her suddenly cling to him, press her lush body against the hardness and heat of his, wanting to lose herself in him, in this heady, needy sensation of entering a paradise she had never known existed.

And the way he immediately deepened the kiss, his answering groan as his hands slid down and urgently shaped the ripe curves of her body, inflamed her so she didn't know what she was doing—until, abruptly, he moved away from her wild embrace. When she could focus at all she saw that she had almost ripped the shirt from his body in her frantic need to feel his skin against hers, his flesh against her flesh.

Portia's face turned bright red with deep mortification and she shuddered irrepressibly. What on earth would he be thinking of her? That she was sex-crazy, anybody's for the asking?

How could she have done that? Oh, how could she? She had practically ravished him on the spot, and if he hadn't called a halt, been turned off by that rapacious response, then goodness only knew what might have happened!

And how could she long so desperately to be back in his arms yet at the very same time wish she was a million miles away? She put a shaky hand to her mouth to stop herself from crying out.

'I'm sorry. That shouldn't have happened.' Lucenzo's voice was flat, but she noted that his fingers weren't quite steady as he slotted the buttons that were left back into their holes and tucked his shirt firmly into the waistband of his trousers.

Swallowing jerkily, deeply and quite horribly ashamed of what she'd done, she looked away from his now silent scrutiny. He was right. Of course he was right. That kiss should never have happened. It had made her feel wonderful, out of this world, but it had created more barriers than it had broken down.

'I'm going in,' she imparted when she could not endure the spiky silence one moment longer. Her voice was stiff with embarrassment as she forced herself forward, treading the maze of paths in an angst-ridden trance.

She did her level best to console herself as she mounted the steps to the sun-drenched terrace. At least what had happened had put an effective stop to the way he'd been insisting on her staying here and had put that dreadfully insulting slant on her motives for telling him she wanted to leave.

And further cemented her decision to do just that.

'This way.' His hand, cupping her elbow, prevented her from crassly, unthinkingly, walking back through the open French doors that led into Eduardo's room.

Disorientated by the mistake she'd been about to make, by the electric touch of his warm hand against her skin, she tried to ignore the way her stomach muscles coiled and tightened. By dint of sheer will-power she managed to pull herself together sufficiently to do her best to freeze him with a look, to pluck his fingers away, one by long, lean one.

Lucenzo stared back at her, a wash of colour creeping along the jutting line of his austere cheekbones, his eyes dark with simmering anger. 'Don't panic. I'm not about to try to have my wicked way with you,' he drawled, and immediately regretted the uncalled for sarcasm as he watched her face go white, the long sweep of her lashes quickly veil her eyes.

Cursing himself for that unfathomable need to lash out at her for rejecting what he'd meant to be a friendly gesture, for acting as though his touch disgusted her, he tightened his jaw in self-revulsion. She had every right to object to what she would possibly see as further unwanted intimacy.

'Come.' He knew better than to attempt to touch her, invade her personal space again, but waited until she fell in step beside him and slowly paced towards the far end of the terrace. He deliberately lightened his tone as he told her, 'I must give you a guided tour some time. You need to be able to find your way around.' To which came no reply.

He really shouldn't have kissed her, he told himself, his thoughts heavy with self-disgust. Heaven knew, it had started out as a simple need to comfort, an instinctive and caring response to the sensitive, hurting side of her, the side that had so genuinely protested against causing any of them any more distress by her being here.

And as a kind of atonement, too. For his former attitude towards her, especially that earlier snide accusation of blackmail.

It had started out that way, as an intention to give comfort, a brotherly peck, a consoling cuddle. But, *madre de Dio!* It had all got wildly out of control. She'd stood, trembling slightly, as his mouth had taken hers, her full lips opening softly for him, like the petals of a rose in the strengthening rays of the sun, and she'd tasted of the sweetest nectar, the headiest wine. It had been then, if he was to be honest with himself, that he'd heard danger signals, loud and shrill, and had decided to call a halt.

But then, right at the significant moment, she'd responded, really responded, and all hell had broken loose inside him. If he hadn't at last somehow found the strength to batten down that raging torrent of lust he would have made love to her there and then, been no better than his brother. Taking and never giving anything that really mattered in return.

Vittorio had inherited his mother's genes, and the inability to love anyone other than himself. While he, himself, had had the ability to love knocked out of him after the death of Flavia, his wife of two short years, and the death of his unborn child. Standing at the graveside, he had vowed never to love again. It hurt too much. Nothing was worth the kind of pain he'd suffered then. Nothing!

He dragged a deep steadying breath. He was not going to relive that time in his head. Life went on.

Leading Portia past the corner of the sprawling villa, down the shallow flight of steps that led to level ground and the path beneath the iron arches covered with tiny, rioting, sweet-smelling roses, would give him enough time to get his head straight.

He had no intention of getting emotionally involved with Portia Makepeace, or any other woman for that matter, and was in no danger whatsoever of breaking the vow that had been so easy to keep for ten long years.

Which meant that touching her again was taboo. So was even thinking about it, because she wasn't one of those smooth, sophisticated bimbos who hung around the rich and the powerful, willing to do anything so long as the pay-off was hefty. She was vulnerable, and mustn't be hurt or betrayed any more than she had already been.

But his need to atone for the hard times he'd given her, for judging her so harshly without asking for her side of the story, coupled with the desire to help her come to terms with the situation she found herself in, had him confiding, 'It might help you to know that whatever feelings Vittorio and Lorna had for each other died a long time ago. They had what is called an open marriage. I don't know about Lorna, but I know my brother had one affair after another. If a woman caught his eye he had to have her, and once he had he quickly lost interest. It was a game to him.'

He shrugged expressively, but his eyes were dark with a mixture of contempt and pain.

He had loved his half-brother, but had hated what he'd seen as Vittorio's moral bankruptcy. 'Naturally, I made sure my father knew nothing of this. He has high moral standards and would have hated to know any son of his could have behaved so badly. And I thank you, Portia, for your thoughtfulness in keeping the way my brother used you from him.'

As they entered the welcome coolness of the marble-paved hallway Portia's soft mouth fell open and the squirm of pleasure in the region of her heart made her feel quite giddy.

Lucenzo believed her! He was actually praising her! His spectacular dark eyes were soft, a deep dark liquid

velvet, and she could drown in them. Trying to break
the mesmeric spell, she lowered her lashes—but her
gaze only dropped as far as his mouth, and stubbornly
stayed there.

Such a beautiful mouth, long and sensual, and she
knew what it felt like: sexy, seductive, utterly capti-
vating. Just remembering that kiss, when she'd promised herself she'd put the whole embarrassing se-
quence of events right out of her mind, made her
shiver in reaction.

Her brain closed down completely when he smiled,
and her whole body was swamped in such a wave of
wicked longing she thought it might quite possibly kill
her! She ran her tongue over her dry and wobbly lips,
but Lucenzo said absolutely levelly, 'Run along.
You've just got time to shower and change before
lunch. We'll be eating in the small *sala*—Paolina will
come and show you where to go.'

Her mind was such a blank she couldn't even begin
to think of all her objections to the awkwardness of
inflicting her presence on the rest of his disapproving
family, and simply did as she was told and took the
stairs like a sleepwalker.

His heart beating unnaturally fast, Lucenzo watched
her go. Kissing her had been a bloody stupid thing to
do, he reminded himself harshly. Kissing her had been
crazy enough, but touching her the way he had, impatient hands urgently learning the lush and achingly
feminine shape of her body, had been nothing short of
madness. It had aroused urges he hadn't felt in a long
time and it might, heaven help him, have created ex-

pectations in her that could bring nothing but disillusionment.

As soon as she was settled here and he could convince her that she and her son were a rightful part of this family—with all the benefits that would bring to both of them—he'd leave. He had legitimate business calls on his time and attention in all parts of the globe. No problem.

His dark eyes brooding, he flung one last look at Portia's slowly retreating back and turned and strode away to find his grandmother.

Nonna would undoubtedly have emerged from the room she'd been given by now, be closeted with her son, telling him in that bracing no-nonsense voice of hers to, 'Pull yourself together, Eduardo. You are too young to be an invalid. I, your mother, will be the first to depart this world for the next—as is entirely natural and as it should be—and I have many healthy years ahead of me!'

Nonna would have to be told to put a curb on that sharp-edged little tongue of hers where Portia was concerned. He, Lucenzo Verdi, would not see her driven away. And the same went for Tia Donatella too—and Giovanni, that spoiled brat cousin of his.

The ferocity of his intentions almost stopped him in his tracks until he edgily reminded himself that he was a fair man, that he wouldn't stand by and see anyone suffer injustice.

It was nothing personal. Too damn right it wasn't!

*   *   *

Portia stood beside one of the open windows in her own pretty sitting room, breathing in the hot, aromatic Tuscan air.

She was on edge and she really knew she shouldn't be, because everything had gone reasonably well. Lucenzo's grandmother had just left the nursery, after inspecting baby Sam and pronouncing him to be adorable and a credit to the family, and Assunta had departed, too, leaving her in peace, with her beautiful sleeping baby and nothing to worry about except how to spend the long lazy afternoon.

Lunch with the family hadn't been the ordeal she'd been dreading. And Nonna—as she'd been told to call her—hadn't looked sneering or contemptuous, except, just briefly, when those bright, intelligent old eyes had first taken stock of the limp, flowered skirt, the well-washed-and-worn T-shirt she'd changed into, the cheap plastic sandals.

She'd asked loads of probing questions about her background during the meal and Portia had answered honestly, because there was no point in doing anything else, conscious that everyone around the lunch table had been listening to what she said.

She was nothing special, she'd said between mouthfuls of what she'd been told was *penne del pescatore*—pasta with lashings of succulent prawns, juicy tomatoes and herbs—which had tasted delicious. She lived in an ordinary semi, she'd imparted, with ordinary, slightly elderly parents and she'd worked as a waitress in a café none of them would be seen dead in.

Though she hadn't said that last bit aloud, of course.

And if they all thought she wasn't fit to belong to the ancient, rich and super-successful Verdi family then tough! She was beyond caring right now. She had other things on her mind.

Like that kiss. What it had meant, if anything. And why it had affected her so cataclysmically when she'd been kissed before—of course she had. But Vito's kisses had never left her feeling as if the whole world had turned upside down.

By the time they'd been served with *macedonia di frutta fresca*—a sort of alcoholic fruit salad she had translated to herself, wondering if she dared plunge her silver spoon into the crystal dish that looked so delicate it might shatter if she even breathed on it— Tia Donatella had unbent enough to ask if she was settling in, and even Lorna, wearing a mauve silk shift today and looking cool and gorgeous, had said, 'I'll show you around some time, help you get your bearings. Just say the word,' managing to sound only the tiniest bit bored by the prospect.

The cousin—Giovanni—had given her a few sly glances which she'd tried to ignore, and Eduardo, whose kind smile she'd missed dreadfully, hadn't been there. He lunched in his room, it had been explained, prior to taking his afternoon rest.

Which left Lucenzo, who hadn't addressed a single word to her. Or looked at her. His sensationally attractive face had looked as remote as the far side of the moon, and the only time he had fleetingly caught her eyes his gaze had been so cold it had made her shiver, making her spill her coffee down the front of her T-shirt in a shame-making brown dribble.

He had acted as if this morning—all those mixed and passionate emotions—simply hadn't happened. So fine, OK, he'd said kissing her had been a mistake and she agreed—well, the sensible part of her did—and she really would try harder to forget it, but what about the rest?

What about the way she'd told him everything, every humiliating detail of her so-called affair with Vito, displaying her own gullibility? He'd obviously believed her and been as kind as he knew how. Was that to be wiped away, too?

Judging from his attitude at lunch, it surely looked that way.

Which was why she now wanted to kick holes in walls!

Catching her fingers practically plucking lumps out of her bottom lip, she sternly told herself to get a life and marched through into her bedroom to change the stained T-shirt for one which looked only marginally better.

As soon as Sam woke and had been fed and changed she would carry him down into the fresh air, she decided, trying to make herself feel sensible and adult. It would be cooler by then, and she'd seen some cute little cotton sun hats in one of the over-stocked drawers in the nursery. He would look almost edible in one of those!

In the meantime she'd sit quietly, making plans. Plans to leave this beautiful, unsettling place. She'd been so right when she'd instinctively known that what had happened this morning had created more barriers than it had broken down. It was more than ever imperative that she should get away.

Two weeks or maybe a little longer, depending on Eduardo's progress, she told herself as she moved around quietly, unable to sit still, tidying the already immaculate nursery.

She had to get back to where she belonged, where she fitted in, where she wouldn't get lost in fantasies of falling in love with Lucenzo—

Falling in love? As if! she mocked herself acidly, rubbing furiously at the sparklingly clean worktop with a teatowel. Of course she wasn't falling in love. No way!

Only a few months ago she'd believed she was in love with Vito and it hadn't been anything like this—this muddled and scary maelstrom of emotions that was plaguing her right now.

It had been calm and comfortable. She'd admired him for the way he had supposedly been struggling to make his way in the world, and she'd worried about him—whether he was working too hard, getting enough sleep, enough to eat. She'd liked it when he'd said she was beautiful, that he loved her and wanted her, and she'd looked forward to their marriage with a warm, contented feeling, because ever since she could remember she had longed for the day when she would have her own home, her own young family.

So what was love? she asked herself scornfully. A wildly beating passion that turned your guts to water and your brains to porridge? Or a fond contentment? It couldn't be both. So perhaps it was neither. Perhaps it didn't really exist outside romantic novels and soppy films!

Getting hot and bothered, Portia told herself that her hormones were playing up. They did, didn't they, after you'd had a baby? That was something she could cope with—wild and muddled emotions because all those hormones were going haywire. They'd settle down sooner or later.

But she wasn't sure about that, not sure at all, when Lucenzo said in that shiver-making dark velvet voice of his, 'I did knock—quietly—but you couldn't have heard. I didn't want to wake the baby if he was sleeping.'

Just his presence made the air around her tingle, hum with a strange prickly tension. She couldn't believe that it wouldn't affect Sam, make him wake up bellowing, but he was still sleeping in his gauzily draped crib, flat on his back with his little arms above his head, his almost transparent eyelids gently closed. Peaceful, innocent, tender.

And Lucenzo was watching him. There was a look on his face that made her heart turn over and a lump jump into her throat. A look that was full of wonder all mixed up with something that looked like pain.

Portia drew air into her cramped lungs, swallowed the awkward lump in her throat and asked thickly, 'Did you want something?'

He turned slowly, as if reluctant to drag his eyes away from the sleeping infant, and when he looked at her his face had been wiped of that puzzling expression. Just blank and remote. His voice was cool as he said quietly, 'A message. Through there?'

He swung his back to her, his shoulders broad and intimidating beneath the silk fabric of his shirt. She followed on leaden legs as he walked through into her sitting room by the door at the far end of the light and airy nursery, glad beyond all reasonableness that he hadn't chosen the other one—the door to her bedroom.

But he wasn't about to jump on her; he'd spelled that out earlier. He deeply regretted those few minutes of passion. He was probably afraid she was about to jump on him—hence that coldly impassive, keep-your-distance expression!

He was all wound up; she could see that. His wide shoulders were rigid, the broad chest that tapered to his slim, flat waist, the narrow hips, the long legs planted firmly apart—all practically screamed tension. Or was it simply wariness?

He could be justifiably wary of her after she'd tried to rip his clothes off! The thought was deeply embarrassing, not to mention depressing.

Hoping she didn't look as bad as she felt—as if she'd been discovered committing some particularly heinous crime—she closed the door to the nursery behind her and asked, 'What message?' Not one he would take any pleasure in relaying, by the looks of him!

'Lorna is to accompany you to Firenze—Florence—in the morning. Alfredo will drive you. You are to choose new clothes.' He stuffed his hands into the side pockets of his trousers as Portia's brows drew together in a frown and her small rounded chin jutted out at a mutinous angle.

'I don't want new clothes. I can't afford them and I won't accept charity.'

Lucenzo sighed. He might have expected this. The woman he had first thought her to be would have jumped at the chance of a whole new wardrobe of designer gear, no expense spared. But the Portia he had come to know over the last few hours, whose story of what had happened between her and his half-brother he believed implicitly because it rang so true, wouldn't take hand-outs.

She had very little in the way of personal possessions, and those she did have looked as if they belonged in a jumble sale. But she had her pride and he respected her for that.

Changing his approach, careful not to make it too personal, he said gently, 'Father and Nonna have been putting their heads together.' He attempted a smile. 'And when they do that, most sensible people run for cover!'

His stab at a smile went unanswered. Portia, he decided, had developed a decidedly stubborn light in her eyes. She had his respect for that, too. But he agreed with every word his father and grandmother had said on the subject—though he could hardly tell her as much, not after those moments of madness this morning. It would imply a degree of intimacy that had to be avoided at all costs.

He tried again. 'You must know that Father already

regards you as one of the family, and he and Nonna
have decided—' he tried to give the impression that
he was searching his memory for the exact words
'—that such a pretty young thing deserves the kind of
clothes that will do her justice.'

'Oh, goodness!' Portia's eyes went wide and her
soft lips parted. How could anyone think she was
pretty when she was only very ordinary? Vito had
called her beautiful but she had been right not to believe him, especially as she now knew everything he'd
ever said to her had been a pack of lies!

Lucenzo forcibly ground his teeth together, to stop
himself blurting out what he felt. She suddenly looked
so bewildered, so achingly vulnerable, it was all he
could do to prevent himself from reaching out, from
touching her, from telling her to believe it. 'Pretty'
was too tame a word. She was an incredibly sexy
woman!

But telling her that would be as good as letting her
know that she had this strange ability to turn him into
an echo of his half-brother—all rampaging male lust!
Just looking at her made everything that was male in
him stand to attention. That silky blond hair falling
around her face, soft strands sticking to her forehead
because of the heat, her huge grey eyes water-clear
and strangely innocent, her too-small T-shirt clinging
to the bountiful perfection of her breasts, her tiny
waist, the curve of her hips that made him think of
feminine fecundity and all that implied—

Closing his eyes briefly, he drew in a sharp breath
and managed, 'Lorna knows the best shops, knows

where the family holds accounts. Please try to accept this gift my father wants to make. Be gracious about it. It would give him so much pleasure to spoil you a little.' And it would ease his own conscience a little, too. So far, apart from his father, the Verdi family had given her nothing but grief.

Portia shifted uncomfortably. When he put it like that she was tempted to comply, if only to humour Eduardo of whom she was already very fond.

But she pointed out honestly, 'It would be such a waste. I won't be here long enough to get much wear out of smart new Italian clothes, and they sure as anything wouldn't fit in with my lifestyle back home!' Then, seeing his impressive jawline go as hard as a rock, Portia mumbled doubtfully, 'Though I suppose they could be left here and I could wear them when I bring Sam back to visit his grandpa.'

The reminder that she was still intent on leaving hit him like a blow to the stomach, emptying his lungs of air. But it was nothing personal. It couldn't be. Hadn't he already decided to take off himself in the not-too-distant future?

He simply wanted what was best for all of them. His father had livened up considerably since meeting Portia and his grandson, and, despite his former opinions, Portia and her little son needed the support of the family. They were entitled to it, after all. Baby Sam was Vito's son.

She was moving restlessly around the room now, her arms wrapped defensively around her body. There was a battle going on inside her head; he was sure of that. The caring side of her, her natural instinct to please, was warring with the side that stubbornly refused to take hand-outs.

There was a tiny frown line between her eyes and a few beads of sweat glistened on the sweet curve of her short upper lip. The desire to kiss away both those outward indications of her inner stress, to fold her in his arms, hold her close, was becoming intolerable. He was going to have to deal with this unwanted and despicable surge of lust in the only way he knew how.

He bunched his hands in his side pockets to stop them reaching out for her and drawled as coolly as he could, 'Don't dismiss my father's generosity out of hand, Portia. I know it would hurt him.' If she was as soft-hearted as he had recently come to believe she was, that should do it. 'I have to leave this evening—business—but I should be back here in a month's time. Will you promise you'll stay, not mention anything about leaving to anyone, until I return?'

He had never had any reason to distrust himself around any woman before now. So the simple solution was to remove himself out of temptation's way before he found himself doing something that would make him despise himself—behaving like his half-brother!

The only indication that what he'd said had had any effect on her at all came in the sudden slump of her shoulders, the way she came to an abrupt standstill and appeared to be studying her feet.

Acutely aware of the waiting silence, Portia grappled with wildly conflicting emotions. He was leaving the villa, and she knew she would miss him so dreadfully that her heart was already aching.

But because she felt so drawn to him, because his mere presence in the same room made a wild sexual assault on her senses, it would be far better if he weren't around, wouldn't it? And without him here it would be easier to stick around for just a little while longer than she'd already decided on.

She lifted her head but didn't look at him as she mumbled wretchedly, 'OK. I promise.'

She heard his quietly voice, 'Thank you.' Heard him leave the room and close the door gently behind him.

And then discovered she was crying.

CHAPTER EIGHT

'BOY, did I need that!' Lorna carelessly replaced her empty espresso cup on its saucer, dabbed her glossy lips with a tissue and leaned back gracefully on her chair, lifting her face to the sun.

She's gorgeous, Portia thought, not for the first time. Clouds of dark chestnut hair, greeny cat's eyes hidden now behind smoked lenses, and a truly enviable svelte, sleek figure.

Quite why Vito had been unfaithful to his elegant wife she couldn't even begin to imagine. And if he'd had to play away from home why pick on someone as ordinary and, let's face it, as dumpy as she was?

Wriggling uncomfortably on her own seat, she cleared her throat and suggested tentatively, 'Alfredo will be waiting to take us back to the villa. Do you think we ought to make tracks?'

In any other circumstances she would have enjoyed sitting at a pavement café table in the sun-soaked Piazza della Republica, relaxing and people-watching—especially after a long and hectic morning being dragged from one exclusive air-conditioned shop to another.

Lorna had appeared to be in her element, but Portia had felt simply awful as she'd been chivvied into trying on masses of things she didn't think she'd ever have the courage to wear. Everything had become a blur of beautiful, classy garments, scarves, shoes and underwear, all bearing designer names she would never in a million years have associated with herself.

Whose idea it had been to dragoon Lorna into accompanying her she would never know and didn't like to ask. It seemed very cruel. True, both Eduardo and Lucenzo had told her that Lorna's marriage had been on the rocks, but it couldn't have been pleasant for the other woman to be ordered to spend what amounted to a small fortune—albeit of someone else's money—on the female who had borne her dead husband's son!

'Let him wait; that's what he's paid for,' Lorna drawled lazily. 'For all he knows we might be in need of a late lunch. Are you quite sure you won't?'

'No, thank you.' Portia's voice was on the strangled side of prim. She didn't mean to sound ungracious but she desperately wanted out of this awkward situation.

She flushed a dull scarlet when Lorna pushed her sunglasses to the top of her head and leaned forward, her cat's eyes level and direct.

'Lighten up. I'm not your enemy, you know. I don't know how long your affair with Vito lasted, and I don't want to. You took nothing from me that I hadn't wanted to be rid of.'

She took a pack of cigarettes and a slim gold lighter from her bag, lit up, and regarded Portia—who was now cringing with embarrassment and guilt—through a blue haze of smoke.

'Vito had dozens of affairs throughout our marriage; he couldn't help himself. Let's face it, it wasn't a marriage made in heaven. He proposed only because after what happened to Lucenzo's wife his father was putting pressure on him, as his second son, to marry and produce an heir.'

She flicked ash into her saucer and then inhaled deeply, giving a slight cynical smile. 'I was socially acceptable—unlike his preferred playmates, the topless models, wannabe actresses, that sort. And I accepted him for his family wealth and connections. We both knew what we were doing, but towards the end I'm pretty sure he was going to divorce me. You see, once I'd got that ring on my finger I'd made it plain I wasn't a breeding machine. Not a maternal bone in my body, I'm afraid. We had endless rows about it— he said I was reneging on our bargain.'

She shrugged and theatrically turned her mouth down at the corners. 'And perhaps I was. We both behaved badly, so I suppose you could say we deserved each other.'

Portia didn't know what to say. It all sounded so callous and heartless. But then she didn't have a sophisticated bone in her body, and certainly couldn't understand how the minds of the super-rich worked.

Maybe this was her opportunity to find out at last what had happened to Lucenzo's wife. Had he divorced because she couldn't or wouldn't produce an heir?

Scowling unconsciously, she twisted her hands together in her lap. He'd left on business this morning and would be away for a whole month. She should be able to stop thinking about him, but she couldn't.

'So—' Lorna squashed the remains of her cigarette in her empty coffee cup. 'There's no need to look so uncomfortable around me—like a scared rabbit trying to find a hole to hide in. I don't bear grudges; life's far too short. Besides, I imagine I won't be around for much longer—a London house to sell, a place somewhere in the sun to buy.'

Her glossy mouth curved in a satisfied smile, then she arched her brows with just a hint of mockery. 'Mind you, you'll have to put up with the aunt and the cousin. They're both fixtures, and they'll probably go on looking at you as if you're an unidentified nasty smell, but you'll learn to live with it. So grab what's on offer while you can. While Eduardo's still around to call the shots. I would, in your shoes. After all, you did what I wouldn't and Lucenzo's wife couldn't— you presented the precious family with the first of a new generation. And, believe me, family comes first with Italians—especially dynastic dinosaurs like Eduardo Verdi.'

With a languid gesture she signalled for the bill. 'Lecture over. I suppose we should put Alfredo out of his misery. We'll come again. You could do with a good hairdresser—silver highlights would suit you— and you need decent make-up. I'll phone around and make appointments.'

Portia wasn't in the least interested in silver highlights or a new lipstick—the only make-up she could ever be bothered to wear. And the moment she could get a word in she asked the question that was now burning holes in her brain. 'What did happen to Lucenzo's wife?'

One finely arched brow twitched upwards. 'I would have thought that old gossip Assunta would have told you by now! Lucenzo wouldn't, of course. He's a cold, unemotional fish, married to the bank.' Breaking off, she settled the bill with a large tip and an even bigger smile for the dishy young waiter.

Portia thought, He's not a fish and he's not always cold. Then went scarlet, thinking of the red-hot passion of those few shared moments.

'There was a time,' Lorna confided, 'before I finally accepted Vito, when I thought big brother might be the better bet. Hunkier by half! I made it pretty obvious—he would have been widowed for around five years at that time—but he wasn't interested.'

The first sign of pique showed in the long greeny eyes, in the snap of the plum-coloured mouth, and Portia prompted, 'How did she die?'

'Flavia?' A tiny shrug. 'It was their second wedding anniversary, would you believe? They were going out to celebrate and he, apparently, was waiting for her at the foot of the stairs. She caught her heel in the hem of her skirt and fell and broke her neck. She was three months pregnant at the time, hence the family's angst.'

She gathered her clutch bag from the tabletop and stood up.

Portia scrabbled for the dozens of classy carriers strewn around the table, wanting to slap the other woman for the callous way she'd described such a tragic event.

Her final throwaway comment was, 'Since then he's let it be known he's not interested in female company—though everyone's guess is he's got a mistress tucked away somewhere. Well, he's got to have an outlet for all that simmering sexuality, wouldn't you say?'

Three weeks later Lucenzo strode down the terrace, leaving his father to enjoy the soft early-evening sun and his lunatic plans while he still could, unaware that the older man was watching him with a wide and decidedly mischievous grin of satisfaction.

Thank God he'd returned a full week earlier than he'd originally said he would. Even another few hours and he might have been too late to stop it. *Gesu!* But his father had run mad!

He plunged into the house by the French windows that led into the rooms his father was using. Inside, he made himself stop to draw breath, try to calm the wild beating of his heart, the internal explosions of emotion. Anger, outrage, something he damned well couldn't put a name to, and yet more anger.

He had to calm down, do what he was best at—think coolly and logically about the problem he was faced with, work out how to deal with it. He had to take stock of the situation.

His father was much fitter now, and the idea of thwarting him wouldn't be the non-starter it would have been a few short weeks ago, so he could put a stop to this nonsense with a clear conscience.

In the three weeks he'd been away Eduardo had

made remarkable progress. No longer gaunt, he was obviously eating well and could get around with the aid of a stick, as he had proudly demonstrated. He was also very full of himself. Too darned full!

Full of Portia and little Sam, too. Wouldn't or couldn't stop talking about them! Portia this—baby Sam that. Portia helped him with his morning exercises, brought him delicacies from the kitchen, persuading him to eat more, and she was on best-friend terms with the staff, all of whom were teaching her Italian. Each day she came and demonstrated her mastery of new words and phrases, and even if they did often laugh helplessly over her pronunciation she was making great progress. And she had—miracle of miracles—even got Lorna cooing over the baby, persuaded her to stay on a little while longer. She also weathered Donatella's barbed comments with good humour and forbearance.

Unclenching his jaw, Lucenzo glanced around the room, airy and bright with daylight and flowers. Her doing, he supposed acidly.

The nurse had been dismissed. She had depressed him, so his father had said, and he was grown-up enough to take his pills on time.

'Grown-up' wasn't what he'd choose to call his parent right now. Stir-crazy was far more apt!

Before he'd been able to get a word in, after the lavish hymns in praise of the supposedly saintly Portia Makepeace, his father had dropped his bombshell.

'She hasn't said anything, but I somehow get the feeling it won't be too long before Portia takes my grandson back to England. I can't put my finger on it, but I think she finds it difficult to settle here. It's understandable, in a way, after what happened between her and Vito, losing him the way she did before he could give their child his name. So—' His eyes had held that stubborn, campaigning light Lucenzo knew so well. 'I will marry her. I will give her and Sam my name. He will be legitimised and she will have my protection, the respect she deserves.'

For long moments Lucenzo had been too shocked to say anything, and when he'd choked out, 'Marry her? At your age?' his voice had been so thick and tortured he had barely recognised it.

'My age has nothing to do with it.' The immediate response had been stern and dignified. 'Portia's standing and security is what matters. And Vito's son has a right to his Italian heritage. Since you decline to provide the family with heirs, am I supposed to turn my back on my only grandson?'

He'd ignored that question. His father knew damn well why he couldn't look to him for an heir! He'd ground out instead, 'Do you love her?' Which had earned him a look of such haughtiness he had known his father was well on the way to complete recovery.

'Like the daughter I never had and always wished for,' Eduardo had retorted at last. 'I don't propose a marriage in the normal sense, but for reasons I hope I've already made perfectly clear.'

Because he thought it was his duty to honour his tragically killed son's intentions?

As Portia had said, and he himself had agreed,

Eduardo mustn't know that Vittorio had used, deceived and betrayed the one woman who'd been gullible and, yes, innocent, enough to trust him. In any case, even if he did learn the shameful truth his intention to protect her would probably be strengthened.

'Have you said anything to her?' Aware that he was clenching his fists, he had forced himself to relax. Were they already betrothed? Was she already choosing her wedding gown? Was he too late to stop this madness?

'No.' Eduardo's eyes had softened, the hand that held his walking stick growing more relaxed. 'I wouldn't dream of approaching her with such a proposal until I had spoken with my remaining son and heard his opinion.' He had smiled then. 'Tell me your opinion, Lucenzo.'

He'd asked for it, so he'd given it him. 'I think you have to be mad!'

Fully aware that once his father had made up his mind nothing would change it, Lucenzo now made his way to his own room, detouring briefly into his study to collect a stiff whisky. He would have to tackle the problem through Portia herself, but only after he'd worked out an approach that would guarantee success. He couldn't afford to foul up; it was too important.

Would she accept his father's proposal, he questioned himself as he showered away the stickiness of long hours of travel, turning his face to the jets of hot water in the hope that the fierce onslaught would clear his brain. Logically, his mind told him that any woman would leap at the chance of marrying into one of the world's wealthiest banking families.

But Portia wasn't any woman, he conceded as he towelled himself dry with a ferocity that dissipated some of the anger inside him. Though why the feeling of rage hadn't died down after the initial first seconds he couldn't quite understand.

Contrary to his first opinion—one that he freely admitted had been cynical and biased—Portia wasn't out for all she could lay her hands on, and it was high time he made his apologies for that.

He'd thought long and hard about it since he'd been away. He believed her version of events, and his insight told him that if she hadn't attended Vittorio's funeral, unwittingly drawing attention to herself, and if that pathetic letter she'd written and his half-brother had ignored hadn't been found, then the family wouldn't have known of Sam's existence. He would stake his life on that.

Worried about his father's state of health, he'd wanted her and Sam to make the villa their home, but the luxurious lifestyle here hadn't tempted her to stay on permanently. Hadn't she already confided that she would be returning to England when Eduardo was stronger? She was sensitive to and caring of other people's feelings and had found her position here as the mother of Vittorio's bastard son more than uncomfortable.

But if her position changed?

As the wife of Eduardo Verdi, with her son legitimised, she would have legal security and the respect not only of their high-ranking social circle but of the local people too. Wouldn't she, if only for her son's sake, agree to the marriage?

And there was another consideration, he thought as he stuffed his severe white shirt into the waistband of his narrow-fitting black trousers. A consideration that made his guts clench into painful knots.

His father was by no means an old man and Portia was generous and appealing and capable of fiery passion, of bringing out the lustful beast in members of the male sex—as he'd discovered to his cost! So how long would the in-name-only marriage remain just that?

The thought was intolerable!

Lucenzo swallowed his whisky in one gulp. He had to see her, talk to her, before his father made that proposal.

Portia exited the bathroom wearing only a smile. Today had been as near perfect as it could get, she thought, hurriedly blanking out the idea that it would have been even better if Lucenzo had been around. It was Assunta's regular day off so she'd had Sam all to herself, apart from the pleasure of sharing him with Eduardo for a few hours this morning. And being in sole charge of her baby had given her the perfect excuse to stay here when Lorna had demanded she go shopping with her.

So Lorna had driven off in a huff, muttering about the stupidity of having offspring because all they did was cramp your style, but Portia had known she didn't really mean it.

Lorna had become her friend, which was pretty amazing, all things considered. And although she never came out and said anything when Donatella made nasty remarks she knew she was on her side—like the time when she'd submitted to Lorna's wheedling and had silver highlights put in her hair and the straggly ends tidied up so that it swung in a smooth bell to her jawline. The older woman had given her one sneering look and said something about silk purses out of sow's ears. She'd ignored her, as if she hadn't spoken at all, but she'd seen the laughter in Lorna's eyes and caught her audacious wink.

But it wasn't pleasant, especially now that Nonna had returned to her own home and wasn't around to keep her daughter in order. And as for Giovanni—well, he was simply a pain. Only this afternoon, as she'd been pushing Sam round the grounds in his buggy, he'd come up behind her, pinched her backside and actually tried to kiss her.

He probably thought that as an unmarried mother she was game for anything! The slap she'd given him should teach him otherwise.

There were rumours among the staff that he was to be sent to the bank's Paris branch to continue his apparently snail's pace rise through the ranks. And if that happened Donatella, as his doting mother, would go with him.

But that wouldn't make any difference to her, because by that time she'd be long gone.

Not that she'd breathed a word of her intentions to anyone. She'd promised Lucenzo she'd wait until he returned and discuss it with him first.

The thought of seeing him again made her stomach turn over and fill up with lot of little jumping, fluttery things. So she would stop thinking of it, of him, stop inflicting this pleasure-pain on herself, do herself a favour and think instead of how to spend the rest of this peaceful evening.

Getting dressed would do for starters, and she rummaged in one of the drawers for clean underwear—daring black satin briefs and a matching bra which made her feel kind of wicked when she wore them. There were several dresses she hadn't yet had a chance to wear, she thought, and she opened the cavernous hanging cupboard door.

The shabby things she'd brought with her were hidden at the end of the rail; the rest was taken up with the sort of clothes most women would give anything to own. It would be a pity to leave them all behind but she couldn't, in all conscience, take them. Besides, they wouldn't suit her Chevington lifestyle. Whoever had heard of a waitress wearing designer jeans teamed with a gorgeous white satin blouse, or a sleek linen suit?

Cutting off a sigh before it could get properly started, she picked out one of the dresses she hadn't yet worn. It was of soft silk chiffon in gently blending diagonal stripes of cream, soft pink and coffee shades, with a slightly flared knee-length skirt and a sleeveless top with tiny fabric-covered buttons all down the front.

Anchoring the final button, she gave an experimental twirl as someone knocked on the door to her suite. Ugo with her dinner tray, though he was rather early.

In the absence of Assunta she wouldn't be joining the rest of the family this evening. When she'd asked Ugo for a tray in her room he'd insisted she use Italian, and after many mistakes, prompting on his part and giggles from both of them, she'd managed it.

'*Avanti!*' she called out, proud of the progress she was making. Most of the staff here spoke some English, but they seemed to have decided that she should learn to speak their language. She'd been happy to oblige them and it was all turning out to be a lot of fun.

But the beaming smile was wiped from her face as Lucenzo entered. Her mouth went dry so that when she managed, 'You're back earlier than we thought,' her voice sounded rusty. His presence hit her like a lightning strike, welding her bare feet to the carpet, sending shock waves through her.

He made no answer, just stared at her from those enigmatically lowered eyes of his. He looked strained and decidedly grim, she thought, and felt her heart swell to twice its normal size in sympathy.

He was a man who had everything anyone could want, yet he had nothing. He'd witnessed the tragic death of his wife and unborn child. Nothing could be more traumatic than that, could it?

Had he shut his emotions away then, or did it go back into his childhood? She recalled what Assunta had told her, how Vito's mother had had him sent away to school because she didn't want him around, how he'd never allowed anyone to see how much he'd minded. Did he sometimes appear cold and unfeeling because he was afraid to show emotion?

Suddenly, she ached to hold him in her arms and cuddle him, take away the pain and loneliness that life had dealt him. Was this what loving meant? Feeling someone's pain as if it were your own, aching to take it away, being drawn to someone even though your logical mind was telling you to keep your distance?

She made a tiny, unguarded sound of distress and saw his jaw clench as his eyes closed just briefly. He opened them again and said, 'I need to speak to you before we join the others for dinner.'

Seeing her again, dressed like that, had practically knocked him senseless. He'd long decided that, somewhat unfortunately for his own peace of mind, she possessed the sexiest body he'd ever set eyes on, but now she had all that plus a very classy beauty. And she'd done something to her hair. It shimmered with light, framed her lovely face with an unruffled elegance. He wanted to run his fingers through it to see if it was real.

To stop himself from even thinking of that very real kind of temptation, he thrust his hands into his trouser pockets just as she stated firmly, 'Assunta's not here so I won't be down for dinner tonight. Ugo's bringing me a tray. Oh—'

A wail from the nursery had her twirling around, her softly floating skirts flying as she sped to rescue her baby.

It wasn't long since she'd bathed, changed and fed him, so he couldn't be hungry. It was probably nothing more worrying than wind, she assured herself as she picked him up, cuddled him against her shoulder and smiled with relief when he gave a windy grin and a great big burp.

Laying him back in his crib after a whole lot of loving chit-chat, she dropped a gentle kiss on each of his petal-soft cheeks and wondered what Lucenzo wanted to talk to her about. The vexed subject of whether she stayed or whether she went, she supposed, dreading having to face his inevitable irritation with her. But, no matter what, she wouldn't change her mind. She was sure now that she was being typically stupid, and falling for him, so that meant that leaving here, and him, was doubly, trebly important.

All of her nerve-endings prickling now, Portia tip-toed out of the nursery and headed for the bathroom to mop herself up, holding the damp bodice of her dress away from her skin.

Ugo glided out of the sitting room and said, *'Buona sera, signorina,'* with his customary wide grin, closely followed by Lucenzo, who stood in the doorway, watching her with narrowed eyes.

Portia watched him watching her and her heart felt as if it might burst. His mouth was a straight, forbidding line and his eyes looked haunted. Did being around Vito's child remind him of his terrible loss? She couldn't imagine what it must be like to watch a loved one die, the two most important people in his world wiped out by a stupid accident.

A sob rose in her throat but she gamely swallowed it. She so much wanted to comfort him, make him happy. But it wasn't in her power. She was fathoms deep in love with him, she admitted wretchedly, but he would never, could never, feel the same way about her.

He had obviously loved his wife so much that falling in love with another woman was an out-and-out impossibility. And even if it weren't he would never take his brother's cast-off.

Portia felt the fine hairs on her body all stand to attention and knew she had to find a way to break this unnervingly strange silence. She moistened her lips. 'You'll be keeping the others waiting,' she said, and her voice sounded strangled.

'No. I used your house phone to give my apologies and ask Ugo to bring supper for two. Which, as you saw, he has done.' Lucenzo knew he sounded wooden and struggled to break free of the trance-like state looking at her had induced.

She was flushed and flustered, her lovely eyes clear, wide and a little too bright, and a pulse was beating madly at the base of her slender neck. One hand covered the thrusting curve of her left breast and he wished his hand were her hand.

He groaned softly. As he knew from experience she could so easily tip him over the edge, and mere animal lust was taboo where she was concerned. She'd had it tough and she deserved better—and he wasn't the man to give it to her. He couldn't give her or any other woman emotional commitment. He'd lived by that rule for a long time now and wasn't about to break it.

He was here in this room, with her, to do a job, he reminded himself cuttingly, not for any other reason. He had to tell her what was in Eduardo's mind and warn her that if she accepted his marriage proposal she'd be making one of the biggest mistakes of her life.

Watching his face close down grimly, Portia shuddered. Supper alone with him would be much too intimate. How could she hope to hide the way she felt? By trying to act as normally as possible, which in her case meant—if her parents were to be believed—like a half-wit! She would start by shutting herself away in the bathroom and getting on with mopping up. The fabric beneath her hand still felt damp.

Grasping the neckline and flapping wildly, she babbled, 'I've got baby dribble on my lovely new dress. I should have stuck to my guns—new mums should wear nothing but charity shop rejects!'

Perhaps he'd say what he'd come for and go.

He did no such thing. Just gave her a long, comprehensive look that made her whole body tingle and her heart pick up speed, beating so madly she thought it might choke her. She gave a long painful shudder as he turned abruptly, stepped into the bathroom and reappeared a second later with a towel. Walking as though he were in a trance, his voice thick, more heavily accented than she'd ever heard it before, he said, 'Here, let me deal with it.'

As he scanned the damp area one hand rose slowly

to slip beneath the neckline while the other dabbed gently with the soft white towel. The backs of his fingers grazed the tingling swell of her breast and Portia sucked in a ragged breath. She felt as if she had walked into the heart of a blazing fire, and colour accented the harsh lines of his cheekbones as his body went taut and very still.

Portia wanted to step away, but her limbs had lost all power of movement and her mind was a total blank. When he raised his heavy lashes and she saw the melting, drowning darkness of his eyes she was utterly, and for all time, lost.

The towel fluttered uselessly to the floor as with a groan of helpless capitulation Lucenzo dragged her into his arms. One heartbeat later his mouth was plundering her and reality spun away.

CHAPTER NINE

THE driven urgency of Lucenzo's passion, his hungry need, inflamed Portia and her own out-of-control wildly emotional responses exulted her. As the yielding softness of her body was welded to the hard male lines of his, her hands flew up to cradle his head, her fingers twining convulsively in the soft dark silkiness of his hair.

The insistent, yet utterly seductive thrust of his tongue was drugging her and her heart was beating to the wild rhythm of blind adoration when he finally broke the kiss. His broad chest heaved as he struggled for air, gathering her even closer as she gave a tortured gasp of loss.

And then he was husking something in his own language and nuzzling her hair aside, his mouth finding the pulse-beat at the base of her throat, kissing her there. Her heart grew wings of soaring joy, her fingers sliding over the breadth of his shoulders then curling into the fabric of his shirt.

He wasn't going to push her away. This time her answering passion didn't disgust him! She shuddered deliciously as his feathering kisses moved lower, down to the neckline of her dress where the pouting swell of her breasts began.

Portia gave a low whimper of pleasure. She felt delirious. She wanted more and more and more. Feverishly her fingers scrabbled at the tiny buttons. She wanted to remove the barrier of fabric, to offer her peaking breasts for his pleasure, for her immeasurable delight, needed to hold on to an ecstasy she had never known existed—needed him, loved him. Loving this man so very much, she ignored the whispery little voice in what remained of her thinking processes which reminded her that she really hadn't meant to fall in love with him at all.

She heard his breath hiss through his teeth and then his hand was covering hers, moving her frantic fingers away from the seemingly hopeless task before slowly, carefully, undoing the buttons himself, parting the fabric and sliding it off her shoulders. His smouldering eyes were intent on the soft mounds of her breasts, intent still while he deftly disposed of the black satin bra, intent until they drifted closed as he bent his head to suckle her.

His whole body was tense, shaking with tiny tremors, and Portia clung to him, her head thrown back, every inch of her on fire for him. Her hunger was savage and uncontainable, so that when he scooped her into his arms and carried her to the fabulous bed she couldn't even think of protesting but cradled his head between her hands again and covered his face with fiery kisses.

Clothes were frantically disposed of. Lucenzo didn't know who had undressed whom. He didn't care. It didn't matter. Nothing mattered but what was happening between them.

Three weeks away hadn't tamed this pagan need, his desire to have her. She was a primitive fever that hadn't attacked him for longer than he could remember. *Gesu!* She was so exquisitely beautiful! So fantastically responsive, generous and willing! What more could any man want?

Her loving arms enfolded him and he gave a throaty groan as his mouth closed hungrily over hers.

Sam's cry woke her. Portia, her mind and body sated, her limbs still boneless with the after-effects of the passion of the night. Struggled feebly within the tangle of sheets. The darkness was thick and velvety, just a tiny glow from the nursery nightlight showing through the partly opened door.

'Wait.' Lucenzo's voice was soft and languorous, and the hand that had been resting on her tummy stroked her there before moving away. 'Stay where you are. I will bring him to you.'

He flicked the bedside light on and Portia struggled up against the heaped pillows, watching him as he slid off the bed, her soft lips parted, her eyes drowsy, dreamy with love. So much love.

Naked, he was utter perfection, and her heart kicked beneath her ribs as she took in the wide shoulders tapering down to the narrowness of his waist and hips, the neat buttocks and long, lithely muscled legs, the olive tones of his skin lightly dusted with dark body hair.

She couldn't believe that such a man could find her desirable. But the way he had made love to her through the night proved that he did, proved that she possessed a streak of wild sexual generosity where he was concerned. Beneath the drugging expertise of his hands her body had become passionately wanton, demanding, enticing, shamelessly willing.

Hot colour stole into her cheeks as he disappeared into the nursery and her baby's cries stopped as if they'd been turned off by a tap. She could hardly believe what had happened. The past few hours seemed like a fevered dream. Quivering with the explicit memories, she put the tips of her fingers to the burning skin of her face, testing for reality, wondering if all this was just a dream, only seeming to be real because she'd wanted his lovemaking so very much.

But it had happened. She was wide awake now. It only seemed like a fantasy because before tonight she had never understood what true, out-of-this-world ecstasy was.

When her conscience had pricked her into spending that weekend with Vito, she remembered—to make their engagement really special, or so he had pleaded—all she had felt was a vague discomfort and quite a lot of embarrassment. Her only consolation had been that she'd made him happy.

Vito had said that wanting her and not having her was driving him crazy. Vito had said he loved her, but he'd lied. Lucenzo had said very little beyond murmured Italian endearments and he hadn't said he loved her. Lucenzo had more integrity; he wouldn't lie.

Sudden tears welled in her eyes. She grabbed a corner of the sheet and scrubbed them away. What sort of woman was she? Comparing one brother with the other. Oh, how shameful! And was she the sort of woman who threw herself into bed with any man who said he wanted her?

Stuffing the sheet into her mouth to stifle a howl of anguish, she mentally tried to calm herself down, to assure herself that of course she wasn't.

Lucenzo hadn't had to say a word. He'd only needed to touch her. And believing herself in love with Vito had been understandable, hadn't it? He'd appeared to be offering her everything she'd ever wanted—the ordinary, simple, uncomplicated things in life because she was an ordinary, simple, uncomplicated creature.

Besides, at that time she'd had no idea what real love was—something dark, dangerous, driven and compulsive, all mixed up with an aching tenderness, a need to give as much of herself as was humanly possible. Like her feelings for Lucenzo.

And what must he be thinking of her now? That she was sex-starved? Anybody's? It didn't bear thinking about, not right now when she didn't feel up to coping with it. With tear-blurred eyes she gazed at the nursery door. The single bedside lamp made the bedroom, this huge four-poster bed, look like a shadowy cave. It was beginning to give her the creeps—and, come to think of it, what was happening through there? Why was Lucenzo being so long?

About to go and find out, she was paralysed by a thought so cataclysmic she couldn't move a muscle.

Neither of them had used any protection. Falling

pregnant by one Verdi brother could be viewed as careless—falling pregnant by two—!

When she'd let Vito make love to her it had been her first time, and she'd naively believed that he would take care of that side of things because although they'd planned to have children that was something that would happen in the future, when they were married and more secure financially. Falling blindly into bed with Lucenzo with no thought of future consequences was inexcusable!

Tears of mortification were trickling down her cheeks when Lucenzo walked back into the bedroom, cradling Sam in his arms. He was actually cuddling the tiny boy, she noted, furiously scrubbing her cheeks, which meant that her baby didn't remind him of the child he had lost, didn't give him pain. And that was something to be glad about, she told herself, giving him a wavery, watery smile as he put her baby into her arms.

'I've changed him for you,' he told her softly. 'And made up his bottle—don't worry, I read the instructions on the formula pack! It's cooling now; I'll fetch it through for you.' He frowned slightly. In the dim light it was not possible to be sure. He leant forward, lifting her chin in his cupped fingers. 'You've been crying.'

There was no way she could deny it and seeing her there, her hair wildly disarrayed around her lovely tear-stained face, her baby in her arms, lit a bright light of sudden inspiration inside him.

He hadn't meant last night to happen, but it had,

and he couldn't regret it. She had been fantastic. He should have been spending the time warning her off accepting Eduardo's proposal. But he hadn't. He'd given in to his baser instincts and made love to her instead, and because of that he now knew exactly what he must do to make amends. And stop his father marrying her and making a fool of himself at the same time.

'There's no need to cry. I don't want to make you unhappy,' he whispered. 'I want you to be my wife. Will you marry me, Portia?'

From the east-facing window of his room Lucenzo watched the sun rise, casting long fingers of shimmering light over the valley. He'd been right to leave Portia to think about what he'd said, he told himself firmly. And that almost irresistible temptation to stay right with her, cajole her into accepting his offer, spend the rest of the night with her, had been a temporary aberration, nothing more.

Spending the rest of the night with her would have meant making love to her again. And again. He wouldn't have been able to help himself. He frowned with deep irritation as heat pooled in his loins and his body surged at the mere idea. The ease with which she aroused his baser instincts quite frankly amazed him, and definitely proved he'd been right to do the sensible thing and remove himself.

He had seen the beautiful logic of his offer of marriage perfectly clearly in that one blinding flash of inspiration. But Portia went with her emotions, not her brain. He could have swept her along with great sex, he was fairly sure of that, but he wanted her to use her intelligence, her logical thought processes, and figure out the advantages of such a union for herself. And that might take some time.

He had too much respect for her to cajole, coerce or seduce her into doing something that might turn out to be wrong for her.

That his father might be furious when he learned he, Lucenzo, had beaten him to it, suddenly occurred to him—provided Portia agreed to marry him, that was. *Madre di Dio!* What did that matter! He'd square it with him, make him see that he was a caring son, shouldering the burden of duty for him!

Running his fingers through his already wildly tangled hair, he stalked through to the adjoining bathroom to take yet another cold shower.

Portia crept back into her own suite feeling dreadfully guilty. She'd smuggled the untouched supper tray for two down to the kitchen, quickly putting the wasted food into the bin, stacking the plates and cutlery and bowls into the dishwasher and making a hasty exit before Cook came in to start the working day.

It would have been truly shame-making if whoever had come to collect the tray had noticed the untouched contents, put two and two together and come up with the right answer!

The news would have been all over the villa in next to no time, and what had happened last night was her secret—hers and Lucenzo's.

Already events were taking on a quality of unreality, and his stunning proposal of marriage was even more unreal—quite unbelievable, really. For ages after he'd left her she'd felt brain-dead!

Puffing from her exertions, she checked on Sam. It would soon be time for his bath and early-morning feed. Disappointed that he was still sound asleep, she pattered back to the bedroom and launched into the task of making the bed look normal, not as if a dozen rugby players had spent the night in it practising scrums.

· That finished, she dragged herself back to the nursery, sitting cross-legged on the floor, waiting for Sam to wake, her head bowed. She really wished she could think straight, make sense of it all. But her mind was numb and shivers of reaction were making her skin come out in goosebumps.

His shock proposal of marriage had been the most tempting, tantalising, wonderful offer in the whole wide world. But she couldn't understand it, no matter how hard she tried.

Much as she would like to believe that he'd suddenly fallen head over heels in love with her, she did have enough common sense—despite her parents' conviction that she didn't have a grain of the stuff— to know that it simply could not be true.

Watching his dearly loved wife and their unborn child die in that tragic accident had traumatised him so badly that the poor darling must be incapable of falling in love again, she thought mournfully, her big grey eyes filling with sympathy.

However, that had been ten years ago, she'd learned. It would be perfectly understandable if he'd met a really beautiful woman now, one who was clever, witty and wise and full of grace, who came from his own social strata, and had finally put the past behind him and found himself falling in love.

But her? Ordinary Portia Makepeace, single mother with no skills to speak of, no graces that you'd notice? It simply wasn't on, no matter how she tried to delude herself into thinking it could be.

And then a truly appalling thought hit her, making her feel nauseous. If she knew anything at all, she knew Lucenzo was a man of integrity. Had he looked at her and decided she was begging for it? And goodness knows she had been more than willing. She had been provocative and, let's face it, greedy! No normal man would have turned down such an opportunity, she thought with deep mortification.

She was a guest in his home, he'd spent half the night having rampant sex with her and they hadn't taken precautions. How could he present his father with yet another illegitimate grandchild? He'd probably felt honour-bound to offer to marry her.

Her wretched body ached with shame, ran with heat and glistened with perspiration, making her thin cotton robe stick to her. And in the midst of her agitated, incoherent cogitations and distracted ponderings over whether to shower and dress, or whether to stay just as she was and shut herself in here with Sam for the rest of the day and refuse to see anyone, the baby woke.

Portia immediately clicked into maternal mode. Wiping her mind clear of all her troublesome thoughts, she rose to her feet, her face wreathed in tender smiles as she reached for her baby. 'Who's Mummy's precious sweetheart, then?' she breathed happily, and enfolded him in loving arms.

Sam had been bathed and fed and was lying on the thick-piled carpet in front of one of the open sitting room windows, looking completely and utterly adorable in a cute blue cotton romper. He was cooing and burbling, strenuously exercising his plump little arms and legs, and Portia was cooing and burbling back at him when Lucenzo walked in, uninvited and unannounced.

Her face turned a shameful fiery red, and all her bones started to quiver at once. How could a man this gorgeous, this powerful, and ridiculously wealthy into the bargain, have spent half the night making love to her and ended up asking her to marry him? It was the most unlikely scenario she'd ever come across!

'Are you all right?' His voice was as tender as she'd ever heard it. He sounded really concerned, Portia thought, dazzled by his physical perfection and shattered by the kindness of his tone.

'I'm fine!' she gasped strickenly. And that had to be one of the biggest lies in the history of the universe! As soon as he'd walked into the room she'd gone back to feeling stressed out, confused and muddled, yet strangely and wildly elated at the same time.

Nervously, she plucked at the edges of her gaping

cotton robe—an attempt at maidenly demureness that seemed hugely hypocritical, not to mention ridiculous, after what had happened in that bed last night, she informed herself miserably.

'Have you given some thought to what I said?'

Portia peered up at him through the hank of hair that was falling over her face, hoping it was hiding her violent blushes. In spite of looking swooningly gorgeous and elegant, in beautifully tailored cream trousers and a toning collarless shirt that deepened his tan and the darkness of his hair and heavily lashed eyes, he had sounded just a tiny bit unsure of himself.

He was probably regretting he'd ever asked her to marry him and was wondering how he could get out of it, she decided sympathetically. The elation, if that was what that strange squirmy feeling had been, drained right out of her, leaving her with everything else: the confusion, muddle and stress.

'No,' she muttered breathily, telling fibs again because she'd thought of little else. 'Not yet.'

Emboldened by the way he hadn't immediately jumped at the let-out she'd handed him on a plate by saying something like, Good, just forget I ever mentioned it, she said squeakily, 'Just because—because of what happened, you don't have to go as far as marrying me.'

'Last night had nothing to do with it,' he stated firmly, sitting in one of the armchairs, looking unfairly relaxed. It was the truth, after all. 'It simply proved that there's pretty strong sexual chemistry between us and that's a bonus.'

'Then why? Why should you suddenly want marriage?' she asked tremulously, and found herself hoping with all her heart—quite probably insanely—that he would now tell her that he loved her and couldn't possibly live without her.

'Well—' Lucenzo rested his elbows on the arms of the chair, steepled his fingers and placed the tips lightly against his mouth. 'If you look at it logically you'll see it makes sense. I married for love once; we were both twenty years old at the time. Two years later I lost her. I have never had the least inclination to fall in love again, hence my continuing unmarried state.'

He slanted her an assessing look. 'Forget romantic clap-trap, Portia, and think about the situation. Free your mind up to see the big picture, if you can. I don't mean to sound patronising, but you and Sam need this family's support. Without it, from what I can see, all you can hope to do is merely survive. True, you can have our support indefinitely by simply staying on here, but in your present position you'd be in a permanent state of limbo. You have already said you find it uncomfortable enough to send you back to England and a life of waiting on tables and worrying about adequate childcare.'

Frowning at the way she seemed to be suddenly afflicted by complete dumbness, because he was sure he'd put the facts precisely and succinctly, he asked, perhaps more sharply than he'd intended, 'Isn't that so?'

'Suppose so,' she snapped back, stupidly hurt because he'd openly stated that being in love with her was the last thing he'd ever think of. 'But you can let me worry about how Sam and I will survive,' she muttered chokily, fighting tears as she saw a fairy-tale marriage to the man of her dreams, a man who loved her as much as she loved him, go down the drain.

'No, Portia, I can't do that.' He sprang to his feet and sauntered over to where she was kneeling, her head sinking down into her shoulders. 'I like you too much, and I respect you. Vito treated you badly and I don't want to see you or your child suffer in consequence. As my wife you would have financial security, respect. On our marriage I would legally adopt Vittorio's son. He would be legitimised and brought up here, as he should be. He would have every advantage,' he stated. 'Surely you can see the logic in that?'

'And what would you get out of it?' Portia asked crossly, swallowing salty tears. 'Why tie yourself to a woman for life just because you're sorry for her?' She wished he'd go away and stop tormenting her. He was looming far too close. She'd got cramp in her legs, if she tried to stand up she'd fall over, and all she wanted to do was to cry her eyes out in private.

But he said, with a trace of gentle humour that made her want to cry even harder, 'I'm not in the least sorry for you, *cara*. I just want to take care of you.' And then he bent down and lifted the gurgling baby in strong capable hands, asking, 'May I take him? Promise you'll think carefully of what I've just said before you join us for breakfast on the terrace.'

And he was gone before she could draw breath to

tell him it didn't need thinking about because she'd already made up her mind.

She wouldn't marry him. Of course she wouldn't. No matter what he thought she wasn't a charity case, and she refused to be treated like one.

Repeating that to herself all the while she was under the shower made her feel slightly better, in control of her life and of her emotions. She dressed in a pair of pale cream linen trousers and a dramatic red silk shirt, and finished off with high-heeled sandals that gave her much needed added height.

To tie herself to a man who couldn't love her when she loved him to pieces would be the cruellest thing she could ever do to herself. Bed would be wonderful; there was no doubt about that. But sexual chemistry wouldn't last if love wasn't there to cement it, so it wasn't enough. Not nearly enough.

Joining the others for breakfast was the last thing she wanted right now, but for some unknown reason Lucenzo had taken Sam with him, and where her baby was she had to be.

Though perhaps his reasons weren't entirely inexplicable, she fretted as she descended the stairs. Hadn't he said he'd adopt Vittorio's son when they married? *If* they married!

Maybe he was already beginning to look on little Sam as his own. Her lower lip trembled. That would be wonderful, all she could want, if only they could form a loving family unit.

But he didn't love her so they couldn't. And that, Portia Makepeace, she scolded herself, is that! She might be a romantic dreamer but she did have her feet on the ground. Well, one foot maybe.

And to prove it she would tell Eduardo of her decision to leave when she saw him later this morning, she decided as she stepped out onto the sunny terrace.

A table had been set beneath the dappled shade of the old fig tree. A sparkling white cloth, bowls of fresh fruit, baskets of bread, jars of honey, tall pots of coffee. And there was laughter, a family warmth she could almost reach out and touch.

They were all there, even Eduardo, who for as long as she'd been here had eaten breakfast in his room. Donatella was holding Sam, her gaunt face wreathed in smiles of pleasure, while Eduardo watched with doting eyes. Even Giovanni was grinning, leaning over to tickle the chortling baby's tummy. While Lucenzo, his back to her, watched over the proceedings.

Portia swallowed painfully and briefly closed her eyes. Like every Italian family, they adored the new arrival. Particularly in this case. Sam was all they had of the lost Vittorio.

Only her pride, her refusal to be seen as a charity case, her fear of seeing boredom in the eyes of the man she loved when, for him, the sexual chemistry he'd spoken of wore off, as it must, was about to deprive her precious baby of all this love, of his Italian heritage.

Back in England his life would be bleak by comparison. Her parents had made no secret of the fact that they resented the intrusion of a baby into their quiet, boring and rather joyless lives. And her own earning power was low so it could be ages before she could save enough to afford to rent a couple of rooms. Then there would be the question of proper childcare. She would manage it somehow, she knew that, but it would always be second best.

Could she deprive her precious son of what he deserved—the very best?

The prickling of his spine alerted Lucenzo to her presence. He turned slowly in his chair and saw her. His heart jumped and his breath came short and fast. Not because she looked so fantastic, though the scarlet of her shirt made her silvery blonde hair look even paler, the figure-moulding light coloured pants bringing back X-rated reminders of last night. And not because she looked strangely vulnerable, excluded and lost. No, not at all.

He pushed back his chair and stood up. This urgency inside him was down to needing to stake his claim before his misguided father attempted to put his own head into the matrimonial noose.

Forcing himself not to rush to her side, he made his pace leisurely. Surely she'd had enough time to recognise the practical sense of marriage to him? Or was she still thinking it over? Was that why she seemed so unwilling to join the breakfast party?

Whatever.

Reaching her side, he said, 'Portia?' and watched her heavy lashes flutter open.

He saw the unusual dullness of those normally sparkling grey eyes and experienced the headiest sense of satisfaction of his entire life when she told him tonelessly, 'I will marry you, Lucenzo.'

CHAPTER TEN

'LUCENZO, my son—you've made me a very proud man!' Eduardo beamed, his dark eyes twinkling. 'Though I'm happy to say I'm not altogether surprised!' He put down his coffee cup and held out his arms. 'Portia, my darling girl, come and kiss your future father-in-law!'

Watching Portia move easily into his father's embrace, Lucenzo narrowed his eyes. He'd fully expected his father to greet the announcement of his wedding plans with a look of downright pique or, at the very least, annoyance at the way his own ridiculous intention to marry the girl himself had been thwarted.

But the wily old devil was genuinely delighted and that 'I'm happy to say I'm not altogether surprised' said it all. Didn't it just!

He, Lucenzo Verdi, acting head of Verdi Mercantile, had been set up! The old man must have gambled on his own unsuitable suggestion of marrying Portia for the honour of the family sending his remaining son off hotfoot to do his duty for him and keep Vittorio's son here, where he belonged!

A smile of wry admiration curved his mouth. Even though this was the first time in his adult life that someone else had manipulated him, instead of the other way round, it was good to know the old fox hadn't lost his cunning! And in all honesty he couldn't regret the way he'd been goaded into making that proposal.

Being married to Portia wouldn't be a problem. She knew the score, he'd been open about that, and she was obviously happy with it and had sensibly settled for the practical advantages of their union.

She wouldn't demand the things he couldn't give her—emotional commitment, protestations of undying love.

His deep involvement in business matters would keep him away on a regular basis, but that wouldn't be a problem, either. Portia was adaptable. She'd proved that when she'd fitted in here, stealing a place in the hearts of his father and Nonna, not to mention the entire complement of staff. Even Lorna had taken to her, now looked on her as an amusing much younger sister. And she would want for nothing. So, yes, Portia would be fine.

And when he was here at the Villa Fontebella he would have the nights to look forward to. Sharing a bed with his wife would be no problem at all!

Portia extracted herself from Eduardo's embrace and shakily took her place at the table. Lorna gave her a friendly congratulatory hug, whispering mischievously, 'Well done, you! You've just landed the most eligible man in Italy!' Which didn't make her feel any better, but more of a hypocrite than ever, in fact.

Donatella, after gently putting Sam into Eduardo's loving arms, gave her a stiff nod and said, her eyes stony, 'Welcome to the family,' then walked back into the villa.

Portia gulped a mouthful of the coffee Lucenzo had poured for her to wash down the lump in her throat. Donatella would treat her with that quelling brand of icy politeness from now on, instead of those acid barbs of hers, but she would never like her. In her eyes she would never become an accepted member of this exalted family.

But she, along with the rest of them, would love and cherish Vito's son. And that was all that mattered, she consoled herself, hoping she didn't look as miserable as she felt.

'*Cara,*' Lucenzo said from behind her. 'Shall we go?' He put his hands on her shoulders, his touch both intimate and reassuring as he excused them to his father. 'Portia and I have much to discuss today. You will have to forgo her company this morning. But under the happy circumstances I'm sure you will forgive us.'

Beyond making any objections, because for one she couldn't really think of any and two she'd used up the last remaining scraps of her mental energy when she'd decided she had to accept Lucenzo for her son's sake, Portia mutely shadowed her brand-new fiancé as he took Sam to Assunta's safekeeping. He instructed Ugo to see Eduardo back to his room and wait with him until the physiotherapist arrived, then ushered her to the rear of the villa, to the garage complex and handed her into an open-topped sports car.

'Where are we going?' she enquired in a small

voice. She quivered as heat ignited inside her—his hand had accidentally brushed against her breasts as he leant over to fasten her seatbelt. This agonising awareness of him had been her undoing almost from the first time she'd set eyes on him, she mourned. Without her being fully conscious of how it was happening it had led her to this unreal situation, as the promised wife of a man who had made no bones about telling her he didn't love her.

'Out,' Lucenzo replied laconically. He glanced at her, his dark brows lowering. There were smudges of fatigue around her eyes, and beneath the soft golden tan she'd acquired while she'd been here in Italy there was a pallor that concerned him. He hoped she wasn't already regretting her decision. 'We need to grab some relaxation before we get swamped in wedding arrangements.'

He turned the ignition key and the engine growled to life. Portia said 'Oh' in a small die-away voice. Another glancing sideways look took in her slumped shoulders, the down-curve of her soft mouth, the limp hands lying loosely on her lap.

She was simply tired, that was all, Lucenzo concluded, his spirits lifting with a surge of relief that took him by surprise.

Of course she wouldn't be regretting her decision. Why should she? It was eminently sensible for all concerned. She'd probably slept as little as he had last night. The recollection of just why neither of them had spent much time sleeping overwhelmed him with a sensation that was entirely primitive male.

When he'd collected himself enough to speak he told her, 'We'll stop off in the village and I'll show you the church where we'll be married.' His voice sounded strangely thick and husky. He swallowed. 'Then we'll head for the hills.'

The short drive through the steep, winding roads brought them to the village, perched high above the valley, and to Portia its fairy-tale quality reinforced the feeling that she was living in a dream, one there would be no waking from.

Lucenzo took her hand and she clutched it gratefully. At least he was solid and real, and her fingers tightened round his as they wandered into the square. It was surrounded by little red-roofed houses and narrow medieval streets. Geraniums spilled from window boxes and the tiny gardens overflowed with courgettes and tomatoes ripening in the hot sun.

Avoiding the ducks and chickens wandering about the square, Lucenzo led her into the church, which was small and austerely beautiful.

'Tomorrow I will start making all the necessary arrangements for our wedding,' Lucenzo imparted unemotionally, glancing down at her when she shivered convulsively. 'You are cold?'

'No.' It was cool in the church, but pleasantly so. Her eyes fixed on the carved pulpit, she asked quietly, verbalising the thought that had chilled her, 'Were you married here—before?' She pulled her hand out of his and wrapped her arms around her body.

There was a slow beat of silence, while Portia battled with an emotion she couldn't put a name to, then

Lucenzo said, 'No. Flavia was Venetian. She was married from her home.' He cupped her chin in one hand, forcing her to meet his eyes, and asked gently, 'Is it important?'

'No, of course not. I just wondered.' Portia's lashes lowered heavily. She couldn't look at him while telling lies. Her own eyes might reveal the truth: that it mattered very much indeed.

He had loved his first wife so much that he still mourned her. No other woman could take her place in his heart. She knew all that, and had accepted it because there was no other option. But that didn't mean she could go through a wedding ceremony, stand exactly where his beloved lost Flavia had stood, and know that when he looked at her he would be remembering the one and only love of his life and making bitter comparisons.

'Perhaps we should get back into the sunlight.' She gave a tiny manufactured shiver, flashed him a smile that was so bright it hurt, and walked to the door with her head held high.

She couldn't afford to let him see how she really felt about him. He would hate it. As far as he was concerned their marriage would be nothing more than a legal contract, with duty on his side and compliance to the family will on hers.

Marriage to a clinging, love-sick loon would be the very last thing he wanted!

'Slow down!' He caught up with her as she stumbled down the steps, taking her hand. 'There is a good *alimentari* on the opposite side of the square—we will take food with us into the hills. You would like that?'

A disarmingly charismatic smile lit his staggeringly handsome features. Portia had never seen him look this relaxed and, yes, happy. The important banker-man on a rare holiday, she divined, melting at once, instinctively giving in to the need to please the man she loved, even if knowledge of that state of affairs was to be kept well away from him.

'Sounds good!' she said, with another sunny smile—one she kept firmly in place as they crossed the square.

Lucenzo paused to exchange a few words with the old women who sat sewing on their doorsteps. They addressed him as *padrone*, grinning and talking so rapidly that Portia, with her beginner's tenuous grasp of the language, could barely understand one word in a hundred.

Standing by while a round little man kept up a joyful running commentary as he filled Lucenzo's order, breathing in the smell of freshly baked bread, coffee beans, cheese and garlic, Portia heard her stomach grumble at an embarrassing volume. Lucenzo's dark eyes met hers, smiling eyes, and she knew his thoughts were the same as hers.

They had both been too preoccupied to eat supper last night, and she wasn't sure about him, but she hadn't touched breakfast, other than a sip of scalding coffee.

It was a moment of intimacy she thought she might

remember for ever, and something ached inside her that had nothing at all to do with lack of food.

Half an hour later Lucenzo pulled the car off the narrow twisting road and Portia, entranced, breathed, 'Oh, Lucenzo—how lovely!'

High meadows overlooked cypress-covered hills, and further down the valley vineyards swept to the edge of the river.

'We will walk a little way.' Lucenzo's arm rested on the back of her seat, and the yearning to lean back, turn her head and taste the tanned, hair-roughened skin of his forearm, was pretty well unendurable.

Her eyes must have given her away, because he gave her a slow, sleepy, incredibly sexy smile and murmured, 'Later. First we walk and then we eat and then...' His eloquent shrug said it all. 'And then we will see.'

High heels weren't the ideal footwear for walking through the long flowering grasses, Portia thought. Or perhaps her knees were still shaking with the effects of what he'd said, the way he'd looked at her, his eyes intent on her face, drifting from feature to feature for long moments, then narrowing as his gaze slid down to rest on the evidence of breasts that were peaking with tingling anticipation against the thin silky fabric of her scarlet shirt.

The second time she stumbled Lucenzo swept her laughingly into his arms and manoeuvred the bulky carrier of food onto her tummy. 'Your legs are too pretty to break, *cara*.' He placed a swift, all-too-brief kiss on lips that were still parted with the surprise of being swept off her feet. 'It is a pity no one ever comes here, not even the most intrepid tourist, to see how manfully I play the hero!'

This unprecedented playful mood made him totally irresistible, so Portia didn't even try. One hand was clutching the carrier, but the other was free to loop around his neck, to drag his head down to claim a kiss that was far from brief this time.

Portia was still breathless and trying to recover from the after-effects when Lucenzo sank bonelessly down in a grassy hollow and held her firmly on his lap. One hand curved round the tight fullness of her breast, the other wound the silky fall of her hair around his wrist, keeping her captive to demands that were made explicit when he fluidly rolled her over and crushed her soft mouth with driven hunger.

What could have been hours or days later, she watched him from beneath eyelids that had suddenly become alarmingly heavy. His breathing was as raggedy as her own and his heart was beating wildly beneath the palm of her hand.

His eyes were liquid with unashamed hunger as his fingers lifted to the buttons on her shirt. They worked deftly, those long, lean fingers, and he was removing the third from its moorings when a terrible feeling of loss overwhelmed her. This was all wrong for her! She pushed his hand away and blurted out feverishly, 'No, Lucenzo!' Looking for something to say to explain her sudden rejection, she added dully, 'I'm hungry.'

'Ah.' He gave her a wry smile, immediately lifting himself off the elbow he'd been leaning on, then turning to hold out his hands and haul her into a sitting position. 'So am I, *bella*, so am I. But my appetite will wait until after we've eaten.'

Sex for the sake of it, she thought dolefully as he reached for the forgotten carrier. 'Appetite' summed it up exactly. Something to be forgotten once it was assuaged. She had imagined she could live with that. It was part of the bargain after all. But now she wasn't so sure. She wasn't sure at all.

Making love with him was more wonderful than she'd dreamed possible, and she wanted him with a desperation that sometimes frightened her. And the wanting would last because she loved him. But he craved her body full-stop. If someone craved cream cakes and gorged on them they would soon be sickened and fancy something else.

Loving him made her too vulnerable to view that situation with anything but dread.

'You said you were hungry.' His darkly probing eyes were intent on her troubled little face and Portia blinked, only now aware that he was holding out a small pancake covered with creamy cheese and a slice of home-cured ham.

She took it because she had to, but she didn't think she could eat, not while her stomach was clenched tight with misery. Somehow she'd gone from one impossible situation to another, and now she was the victim of her own needy love for this man, of her fierce maternal desire to do the very best for her son.

Lucenzo reached out and touched the side of her face, a gesture so tender it made her want to cry because it hadn't stemmed from love. He wanted sex with her. That was what this was about.

'Portia, what's troubling you?'

Her eyes lifted unwillingly to his. There was definitely something wry about the smile that hovered around his sensational mouth. He'd brought her here to have sex with her, away from prying eyes and clacking tongues back at the villa. That was all she was good for, apart from satisfying his family honour.

And now he would think she was behaving like a sulky, temperamental child, denying him what she had so freely offered last night.

Her sigh came up from the soles of her feet. She laid the unwanted food on the paper napkin Lucenzo had provided and pushed her hair away from her face with the back of her hand.

'I feel trapped,' she told him honestly, and if this was the beginning of a conversation that would lead to him freeing her from her promise to marry him, then so be it, she decided fatalistically. 'I feel like a puppet. People are pulling strings and I'm making the right movements because I don't have any choice in the matter.'

'You are no wooden doll, Portia.' His voice was an unashamedly sexy purr. 'You are a warm, flesh and blood woman and you give me much pleasure!'

'Sex!' she snapped, tugging out clumps of grass without being aware of what she was doing. Sometimes he got her so angry!

She was angrier still when he came back with that

lazy, heart-breaking grin of his. 'And what's wrong with that? I think you enjoy it, and I know I do!'

She pulled her knees up to her chin and wrapped her arms around them, giving him a sideways glare.

'Do you always take people this seriously?' she enquired with a bite of sarcasm. 'Or is it only me?' She could strangle him sometimes, she really could!

'Ah,' he intoned slowly. 'Right.' He reached out his hand and gently touched hers. 'I'm sorry,' he told her seriously. 'Tell me why you think you're being manipulated. Who is pulling your strings? I want you to be honest about your feelings.'

Portia immediately felt weary and tearful. When he looked at her with such kindness in his dark, liquid eyes it did her head in and just made her love him all the more. It was far easier to be angry with him.

There was no way she could be completely honest and tell him how deeply she loved him, but she could tell him something. 'Vito knew all the right strings to pull. And my parents—they made it as good as impossible for me to refuse your father's invitation to bring Sam out here. And your father himself—he doesn't mean to put pressure on me to stay, but my knowing how besotted with Sam he is, how much happier and stronger he's getting, does it for him. And then—' she shot him a baleful glare '—there's you. With all those sensible reasons why we should marry. If that's not manipulation, I don't know what is!'

Her voice had risen to a wail and a solitary tear glistened on her cheek. Lucenzo wiped it away with the ball of his thumb. 'You could have refused me,' he pointed out gently. 'You had that choice.'

'Some choice!' Portia retorted fiercely. 'The choice between my baby being brought up back in England—merely surviving, as you pointed out yourself, around grandparents who regret his very existence—or being here, with everyone doting on him, having every possible advantage. What kind of choice is that?' she demanded chokily, then lowered her head in abject misery as she confessed sorrowfully, 'As usual, I took the coward's way out.'

Lucenzo closed his eyes. Crunch time. He could truthfully tell her that if she opted to return to England, taking Sam with her, then of course both of them would be handsomely provided for. The Verdi family took care of its own.

But surely she would be happier here. Eduardo loved her like a daughter, and he would miss her and his grandson so much that his excellent progress might be reversed. That was as good a reason for her continued presence as anything he could think of.

And, he admitted, registering a peculiar lurch in the region of his heart, he'd got quite used to the idea of remarriage. Especially when his future wife was so warm and sexy. He quickly dismissed his lustful motives. In any case, she needed to be grounded, to have someone responsible to look out for her.

Her heart was definitely in the right place, but she was inclined to be a little scatty, not to mention impulsive. The combination might be oddly endearing, but it could also lead to unscrupulous people—like Vittorio, for example—taking advantage of her.

No, she definitely needed looking after. And he was the man to do it.

He said, not quite levelly, 'You made your choice and it was a courageous one. You agreed to spend the rest of your life with me for your son's sake, when for all you know I could be a wife-beater, unfaithful and neglectful.'

He took both her hands in his and lifted them to his mouth, kissing the backs of her slender fingers. 'I give you my solemn promise that you will never regret our marriage. I will be loyal throughout our lives, and while I draw breath nothing will harm you. *Cara*, I care about you—' His voice broke as the knowledge hit him like a ton of bricks. *Madre di Dios*—he loved her!

After what had happened to Flavia he had vowed he'd never leave himself open to such hurt again. But it had happened. He loved everything about this woman. The beauty of her smile, the way she had of putting others' needs before her own, the sweet vulnerability that lit such an unquenchable spark inside him, her open, generous nature.

He felt his body tremble, his heart open and flower. Taking her hands, he looped them around his neck and cupped her sweet face with his own slightly unsteady fingers.

It would be a mistake to tell her how he felt. She wouldn't want the responsibility, the burden of his love, when there was so much else for her to come to terms with.

But he could, in time, teach her to love him. This wasn't about his father's or her child's best interests. It was about what he felt for her. And he could tell her, with almost vehement sincerity, 'Trust me, Portia. It will be all right. It will be perfect, I promise you.'

CHAPTER ELEVEN

'WHICH one suits me best, Nonna?'

Portia, her cheeks the colour of pink roses, her grey eyes sparkling, made a stately perambulation of her sitting room.

'This, or one of the others? Goodness,' she giggled, 'I feel like a professional model prancing down the catwalk—though I guess I don't look like one! Do I look too bosomy?'

'That one,' Lorna piped up in the background.

Lucenzo's grandmother put her aristocratic head on one side and said, 'I agree. That is perfect.' Then she clapped her hands together. 'You are perfect. Oh, I do love weddings!'

'*Si, si! Bella, bella!*' Assunta cried, and even little Sam, jiggling in her arms, gave a crow of excitement.

At nearly four months he was developing quickly. Portia gave him a love-drenched smile. In one week she would be marrying to secure his future and there were no regrets.

Her husband-to-be didn't love her, of course, but she could live with that because she knew without a question of doubt that he really cared about her. Hadn't he said so? Promised to be faithful to her? And the way he'd made love to her, that day in the high

meadow, had even transcended the wild passion of the
night before. It had seemed deeper, more meaningful.

Realising her flush was deepening to a vivid blush,
she returned to the mirror. Lucenzo had arranged for
a selection of wedding gowns to be flown in from
Milan, and although they were all lovely, and she really was spoiled for choice, she had to agree that this
one made her look like a fairy-tale bride.

Fashioned of ivory-coloured wild silk, the bodice
fitted like a second skin. The deep neckline showed a
discreet amount of cleavage, and the rustling silk skirts
flowed down from her tiny waist. The long, narrow
sleeves, which were fashioned from delicately em-
broidered lace, echoed the filmy veil.

'I have something for you,' Nonna said, hauling a
velvet-covered box from beneath the chair she was
occupying and opening it to display a glittering dia-
mond-encrusted tiara resting against dark blue satin.
'It belonged to my great-grandmother and has been
worn by Verdi brides ever since. Perhaps you would
try it now? And then we will have Ugo lock it in the
safe until your wedding day.'

Portia's eyes went very wide as she gazed at the
incredibly delicate jewels. 'Are the stones real?'
Goodness, what a responsibility if they were!

'But of course.' Just for a moment aristocratic
haughtiness looked out of her eyes, centuries of breeding. 'Verdis do not wear paste.' Then she smiled imp-
ishly. 'My great-grandfather bought it for his bride-to-
be in St Petersburg. It was already very old. He was
a man of great good taste.'

'I was a Verdi bride,' Lorna pronounced sulkily as Portia gingerly fixed the glittering tiara. 'How come I didn't get to wear it?'

'Because, my dear—' the old lady's level look was not unkind '—yours was not a true love match. Anyone with a grain of sense could see that. And I have more sense than most and a nose for such matters. The Verdi men have always married for love. In the case of your marriage to Vittorio the wearing of such a love token seemed inappropriate.'

Portia gazed at the starry glitter on her head and was swamped with guilt.

Her Verdi man wasn't marrying her for love. Surely if Nonna had 'a nose for such matters' she must see that? Or had her venerable age robbed her of her judgement?

With such an apparently long tradition behind the tiara she would feel a fraud if she wore it. With trembling fingers she laid it back in its box, hoping that when the big day came Nonna would forget all about it and leave it safely locked away until it could grace the head of a Verdi bride who was truly loved.

'Shall we sit awhile?' There was a stone seat in the shade just inside the enclosed garden, where old roses bloomed in a wild and perfumed tangle, their exuberance grounded by the formality of pencil-slim cypress trees.

'Oh, Eduardo—have we walked too far?' Portia shot him a worried glance. 'Are you exhausted?'

'Not a bit of it—don't fuss! I want to talk to you, that is all.'

'Right.' Portia angled the buggy further into the shade. Sam was blissfully asleep and would probably stay that way for another hour. A quiet few minutes in this beautiful place before they headed back to the villa through the gardens was just what she needed.

Eduardo was wearing a battered panama, a straw-coloured linen jacket and he looked as fit as a fiddle. So she really shouldn't worry about getting him over-tired. Since Lucenzo had told him of his marriage plans three weeks ago his progress back to full health had been remarkable.

'Everything is in hand for the big day?' he asked as Portia settled beside him. 'And the marquee is going up tomorrow? Is that woman Lucenzo hired to organise everything doing her job properly?'

Portia gave him a beaming smile. He was such an old darling! He knew the answers to all his questions before he asked them. He and Nonna had demanded to be kept abreast of every tiny detail from day one.

But she was happy to humour him. Talking about the wedding made it seem more real. Mostly, she felt as if she were living in a dream. 'Signora Zanichelli's doing a brilliant job. The flowers, the music, the ca-terers—everything is arranged. And all the people on the guest list you and Nonna gave her have replied in the affirmative.'

'Good. Good.' He nodded his satisfaction. His hands were resting on the top of his ebony walking cane which he carried, Portia suspected, more for effect than practical purposes. 'And your parents arrive when? I am looking forward to meeting them.'

'The day after tomorrow, two days before the wedding.' As he knew very well! Did he, too, keep going over the details just to convince himself it was all really happening? She was looking forward to seeing her parents again, even though her mother's reaction when Portia had phoned hadn't been flattering.

'Why?' she had asked after a stunned silence. 'Why on earth would a man like him marry a girl like you?'

'My son returns this evening,' Eduardo remarked as Portia pondered her mother's habit of cutting her down to size. 'He works far too hard. You must try to curb that tendency when you are married.'

'Lucenzo will do what Lucenzo wants to do,' she answered lightly, to cover the nagging little worry that kept plaguing her.

She had seen nothing of him for the past three weeks. He was away on business and she missed him so badly she sometimes didn't know what to do with herself. He phoned her each evening, but that was just for the sake of appearances.

If long and frequent absences were to be the pattern of their future life—growing longer and more frequent as the sexual chemistry wore off for him—she didn't know if she'd be strong enough to keep on pretending to be a happy, understanding wife.

'When a man adores his wife he will do anything to please her,' Eduardo opined.

'Perhaps,' Portia concurred. Generally speaking, she supposed he was right. He wasn't to know that

Lucenzo didn't love her at all. He might be fond of her, and lust after her whenever he was around long enough to do anything about it, but that was as far as it went.

Happily unaware of her train of thought, Eduardo confided, 'Lucenzo stopped grieving for Flavia many years ago. But after her death he locked the door of his heart. That was understandable at that time, of course. But he forgot how to open it again and that was deeply regrettable. Then you came along and opened that door. I saw it happen and was happier than you'll ever know. But my son is stubborn and his emotions had got so rusty he didn't know how to trust them. So I gave him a push!'

'A push?' Portia didn't know what he was talking about, but she did know he had seen what he wanted to see—his remaining son falling in love and marrying again. Didn't everyone want to see their children happy and settled?

Eduardo patted her hand, his eyes bright, his smile loving. 'You are my daughter now, and there will be no secrets between us. When I was sure of the way he felt—even if he didn't know it himself at the time—I told him one great big untruth!'

He threw back his head and laughed unrepentantly. 'I told him I was about to ask you to marry me! Family honour had to be satisfied, Vittorio's child legitimised and made secure. The look on his face! My dear, I don't know how I managed to look serious and determined! He was off like a bullet from a gun—it was just the shock he needed to show him his true feelings and make him propose to you himself before his silly old father could get a word in! I shall confess this to him later—this evening after dinner, perhaps. I want there to be no misunderstandings between any of us. I feel very proud of myself for bringing the two of you together.'

Portia made a big production of looking at her watch, checking on her baby. She said gently, 'I think we should be getting back now.' She managed a smile, but it felt wooden. If Eduardo thought that what he'd just told her was romantic and would please her he was very wrong. It simply made everything that little bit worse.

When she'd tried to figure out the reason behind Lucenzo's proposal—which had literally stunned her—she'd drawn the conclusion that after the night that had proved they were sexually compatible he'd decided he might as well marry her and be done with it. A more than willing body in his bed, a certain fondness, the formal adoption of his brother's son. The package made sound sense.

But it hadn't been like that, had it? He had come to her room that night with the express intention of proposing marriage. Even if she'd been truly ugly, with no teeth, three legs and a hump, he would have gritted his teeth, closed his eyes and taken her to bed. Then proposed to her because he loved his father and was worried about his health. He would have done anything he could to save him from the hassle of marrying a woman who was young enough to be his granddaughter!

It was a demeaning and very sobering thought.

* * *

Portia was getting ready to join the family for dinner when Assunta arrived to babysit.

'Lucenzo has just got home,' she said excitedly. 'He asked me to tell you that he is going to say hello to his father before changing and he will see you at dinner—which will be put back half an hour on account of his being held up. That is a very smart dress you are wearing.' She tipped her head on one side and said, not altogether approvingly, 'Black makes you look older. Oh, and don't forget your ring. The last time I saw it it was by the kettle in the nursery.'

Portia had taken it off as soon as she had returned from talking with Eduardo, just before lunchtime. The square-cut diamond in the heavy antique setting had seemed so false, signifying nothing. She made a mental note to ask Ugo to lock it in the safe, along with that tiara—the thought of wearing that glittering symbol of undying love had been haunting her for days— and turned to the mirror to brush her hair.

Assunta was right, she thought as she studied the reflection of the severely cut black silk sheath dress. Black suited her mood. And she felt older. But was she any wiser? She doubted it. Wisdom flew out when love walked in. Everyone knew that.

And her heart shouldn't have sunk to the level of her pretty new shoes on hearing that Lucenzo had made seeing his father his first priority.

He loved his father. He didn't love her. What Eduardo had told her this morning shouldn't make a scrap of difference. She was still committed to marrying a man who would never love her for the sake of her son.

She walked listlessly from the room. In any other circumstances she would have joined Assunta in the nursery, passing the time in chatter, practising her Italian. But tonight she needed to be on her own.

Would Lucenzo kiss her and tell her how much he'd missed her? Probably. He'd be putting on an act for the sake of the family gathered around the dinner table.

Could she take it, knowing it was a sham? Or would she push him away, discarding the act for the sham it was, just as she'd discarded the ostentatiously valuable engagement ring he'd given her?

She really didn't know and she needed time to think about it. It would be cool on the terrace; she could be on her own.

But even that was denied her. Silently mounting the steps beyond the rose arch, she saw that Donatella and Lorna were already seated at the table where the family often took *al fresco* breakfasts. They had long drinks in front of them. Portia would have retraced her steps, gone further into the gardens, but Donatella's acid-toned voice stopped her.

'I don't know how I'm going to face my friends at this farce of a wedding. Lucenzo Verdi marrying that common little nobody! He wouldn't have given her a second glance in any other circumstances. A mere waitress who sleeps around—I ask you! We all know why he's doing it, of course. He always was a clever devil. He'll marry the creature, adopt Vittorio's son to make everything legal and above board and then get rid of her. He'll pack her back to England with nothing but the rags she came in, and keep that poor little boy out of her clutches.'

Leaning back in the shadows, Portia felt sick. She knew Donatella disliked her, but why would she invent something like that? They were a close-knit family. Had Donatella told her nephew, Lucenzo, that she strongly disapproved of his wedding plans? And had he, to put his aunt's mind at rest, told her of his real intentions?

Her ears straining, she waited to hear Lorna tell the older woman not to be a fool, that Lucenzo would never do something so callous and cruel.

But Lorna merely laughed.

And that cold, tinkling sound echoed in her ears as she turned back the way she had come.

Assunta glanced up from her knitting. 'You've come back for your beautiful ring—didn't I tell you not to forget it!'

'No.' Portia was trying to hold herself together. All her insides were shaking and her legs would barely hold her upright. She tugged in a ragged breath. 'Perhaps you'd let them know I won't be joining them for dinner. I've developed a migraine and—'

'You poor child!' Assunta was on her feet, her knitting cast aside, peering at her. 'You don't look at all well. What can I get you?'

'Nothing.'

'Pills? A glass of water?'

'No. Really.' Portia would have liked to tell her to go away, but she couldn't be that unkind when the older woman was so genuinely concerned about her. 'I just need to lie down quietly for a little while and then it will pass. Truly.'

'Then I will sit here while you rest. To look after the little one should he wake.'

Portia closed her eyes, fighting for control. She was nearing the end of her tether; she could feel it! She had to be alone to do what was necessary. She said as calmly as she could, 'Please, Assunta. He won't wake for a while, and when he does I can manage. Just pass my message on. Please.'

For a few agonising moments she thought the older woman was going to argue, but thankfully at last she left, and Portia methodically changed out of her dress and into her cotton robe.

She couldn't stay. Not if there was the tiniest risk that what Donatella had said was true. She would get over her love for Lucenzo in time, but she would never survive if he married her, cast her aside and took her baby from her.

There was no sign of the battered suitcase she had arrived with. Paolina had probably burned it. But there were still two of the classy carriers left over from her shopping trip tucked away at the bottom of the hanging cupboard. It took only moments to fill one of them with the things she'd need for Sam on the journey back to England tomorrow.

Their passports and her UK currency were still in the drawer where she'd put them for safe-keeping all those weeks ago. Not letting herself think about anything but the task in hand, she transferred them to her old handbag and started to push the clothes she'd brought with her into the other carrier, leaving out a pair of old jeans and a T-shirt to wear in the morning.

She draped them over the back of a chair to put on as soon as she woke in the morning. If she ever slept. But she wouldn't let herself think about the long, empty hours of the night. She just had to carry on with what she was doing. She couldn't afford to let go.

But she almost did just that when Lucenzo walked into the room. Her breath locked in her throat and she started to shake, raw sobs building up a terrible pressure inside her. The carriers dropped from her nerveless fingers. So tall, so dark, so outrageously attractive, how was she going to stop loving him, needing him?

'Assunta said you were unwell.'

How could he look so concerned when he really didn't give a damn? When he only wanted custodial rights over her son?

'What are you doing?' Narrowed eyes fastened on the carriers, his frown deepening. A sleeve of that awful home-made dress, the one he'd made her wear for that first dinner with the family, was hanging out of one of them. He could hardly miss the connection.

In any case, she had to tell him.

'There will be no marriage, Lucenzo. Sam and I will be leaving in the morning. If you can spare Alfredo, could he drive us to the airport?' A sudden feeling of guilt swamped her. A lot of time, trouble and money had been spent on the wedding arrangements. And all those lovely clothes everyone had insisted she have. Thinking of the waste made her feel dizzy.

Lucenzo's strong face clenched. He asked tightly, 'What is all this about?'

'It's about the way everyone knows—except Eduardo, because he's far too nice to go along with it—that you're going to adopt Sam when we're married. Well, I knew that, of course, but I didn't know you planned on throwing me out and keeping him!'

She had blurted it out without thinking, and immediately wished she'd kept her mouth shut when he countered with a decisive bite, 'Who is "everyone"?'

Portia kept her mouth tightly shut this time. Though it was a bit like shutting the stable door after the horse had gone, she thought miserably, visibly shaking now.

She didn't want to cause bad feeling between members of the family. Donatella couldn't help disliking her and taking comfort from the thought of her coming downfall. Lucenzo's aunt was a dreadful snob, but that would be down to the way she'd been brought up and not really her fault.

'Sit down before you fall down.' He helped her into a chair, the one she'd draped her old jeans on. He was quite gentle about it—probably because her teeth were chattering now and he feared a noisy descent into hysterics—but he looked blackly furious.

Because she'd learned of his intentions before it was too late?

Or because his character had been so badly maligned and the woman he was supposed to be marrying didn't trust him one little bit?

Whatever, there was no future for them as a couple now.

'Portia, who gave you that ridiculous information?' he asked with predictable ferocity. 'I need to know.'

A tear slid down her cheek.

Lucenzo visibly reined himself in, hunkered down in front of her and took both of her hands in his. 'Tell me,' he insisted quietly. 'I think I know who's been telling you lies, but I need you to verify it.'

Portia blinked rapidly. She wished she didn't cry so easily. She would have loved to think that what Donatella had said was wicked lies, and if Lucenzo's aunt had said all that to her face she would have had no difficulty in putting it down to sheer spite. But she'd been talking to Lorna. She'd had no idea anyone else had been listening in.

'Who do you think?' she asked in a shaky voice, stalling, quivering inside as he brushed her tears aside with his fingertips.

'My dear Zia Donatella, at a guess,' he said heavily. 'I'm right, aren't I?'

Portia nodded speechlessly. Then, at the wry twist of his mouth, she managed, 'I overheard her talking to Lorna. If she'd said such things to my face I would never have believed her. I would have put it down to spite. She's never been able to like me.' She gulped frantically. 'She once called me a sow's ear. Is it true?'

'You look nothing like a sow's ear.' His dark eyes gleamed and his mouth twitched unforgivably.

Goaded, Portia wailed, 'I meant the rest. And it's not funny!'

'Of course it's not true!' he snapped out tersely. 'Heavens above—what kind of monster do you think I am?' Then, seeing her soft mouth crumple, he groaned, driven. 'I'm sorry. Why would you trust me? I treated you badly to begin with, accused you of practically everything under the sun, and for that I apologise.'

'Belatedly,' she pointed out—although she'd forgiven him ages ago, because he'd changed completely once he'd heard her side of the story regarding what had happened with her and Vito.

'Touché!' He took her hands again. 'Portia, listen to me. Zia Donatella is a mean-minded woman. Those things she was saying were probably wish-fulfilment. She would never have dared to say such things to your face because you would have reported back to me. Then she would have had me to deal with. And that, believe me, she would not like! Tomorrow morning she will be out of this house. She will not be at our wedding.'

At his softly tender expression a great dam burst inside her. For a split second she thought she could control it, but then she knew she couldn't.

'I can't marry you, Lucenzo!' she wailed. 'I kept telling myself I could. For Sam. For your father. And everything. I guess I'm being really selfish—'

Tears were pouring unstoppably and she was having trouble getting any words out. But she had to make him understand, even though he was making things a thousand times worse by looking completely and utterly shattered by what she'd said already.

'I'm thinking only of myself, and I know I shouldn't, but I can't go through with it. Please try to see! Oh, Lucenzo, don't you understand? I might love you but it isn't enough. I need to be loved!'

She was sobbing so convulsively that she didn't have the strength to resist when he stood up and pulled her into his arms. She could only cling to him and soak the front of his shirt.

When she'd reached the noisy hiccuping state she heard him ask, 'Did I hear right? Did you say you loved me?'

It was exactly the sort of shock she needed to cure those hiccups. Had she really said that? She supposed she must have done. She hadn't meant to.

'Did you?' he prodded.

Portia nodded and mumbled, 'Yes. Sorry. I know you don't love me. And I also know the only reason you asked me to marry you at all was because your father told you he was going to ask me. But don't worry about it. I understand why you did it.'

After a short silence while he unravelled the tangle of what she'd just said, and after what Portia suspected was an inner rumble of laughter, Lucenzo whispered against her ear, '*Carissima*, you know nothing. I was horrified when Father told me what he intended, and I came to your room that night to warn you, to tell you that you'd be making the biggest mistake of your life if you were to tie yourself to a man so much older than yourself. I was too cowardly to analyse my own emotions and I ended up making love to you instead. That was when I decided I wanted to marry you. And

I was still being a coward—telling myself I'd never love again—because I was afraid of being badly hurt.

'I was behaving like a fool. An even bigger fool when I had to be honest with myself and admit that I loved you, adored you. I'd banked on making you fall in love with me after we were married. Now—' he pushed her rumpled hair back off her face '—we will have no more talk of cancelled weddings. I absolutely forbid it. I love you. You love me. We will be perfect together. And before you drown me in tears, I am going to phone down and ask Ugo to bring a tray of food. And champagne. And this time,' he drawled softly as he gazed lovingly into her glittering eyes, 'maybe we will get to taste just a little of it!'

The ceremony had been beautiful: the little church packed to overflowing, the square crowded with the villagers who hadn't been able to squash inside.

There were flowers everywhere, and waving people lining the road back to the villa, ready to follow on foot, by bicycle, on mule-drawn carts to enjoy the reception, because everyone had been invited.

Sitting with her brand-new, endlessly fascinating, shatteringly handsome husband in the back of the flower-strewn chauffeur-driven Bugatti drophead, the Verdi tiara glittering in the sunlight, Portia returned the waves and smiles ecstatically. She almost swooned with a happiness that seemed too great to contain in one mortal body when Lucenzo took her in his arms and to a great roar of crowd approval kissed her very soundly.

And she knew exactly what he meant when he tucked her bright head against his wide shoulder and whispered, 'I am jealous of all these people, my beautiful darling. How soon do you think we can slip away?'

The world's bestselling romance series.

HARLEQUIN®
Presents

Seduction and Passion Guaranteed!

A new trilogy by Carole Mortimer

BACHELOR COUSINS

Three cousins of Scottish descent...they're male, millionaires and marriageable!

Meet Logan, Fergus and Brice, three tall, dark, handsome men about town. They've made their millions in London, but their hearts belong to the heather-clad hills of their grandfather McDonald's Scottish estate.

Logan, Fergus and Brice are about to give up their keenly fought-for bachelor status for three wonderful women— laugh, cry and read all about their trials and tribulations in their pursuit of love.

To Marry McKenzie
On-sale July, #2261

Look out for:
To Marry McCloud
On-sale August, #2267

To Marry McAllister
On-sale September, #2273

Pick up a Harlequin Presents novel and you will enter a world of spine-tingling passion and provocative, tantalizing romance!

The world's bestselling romance series.

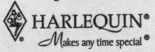

If you enjoyed what you just read,
then we've got an offer you can't resist!

Take 2 bestselling love stories FREE!

Plus get a FREE surprise gift!

Clip this page and mail it to Harlequin Reader Service®

IN U.S.A.
3010 Walden Ave.
P.O. Box 1867
Buffalo, N.Y. 14240-1867

IN CANADA
P.O. Box 609
Fort Erie, Ontario
L2A 5X3

YES! Please send me 2 free Harlequin Presents® novels and my free surprise gift. After receiving them, if I don't wish to receive anymore, I can return the shipping statement marked cancel. If I don't cancel, I will receive 6 brand-new novels every month, before they're available in stores! In the U.S.A., bill me at the bargain price of $3.57 plus 25¢ shipping & handling per book and applicable sales tax, if any*. In Canada, bill me at the bargain price of $4.24 plus 25¢ shipping & handling per book and applicable taxes**. That's the complete price and a savings of at least 10% off the cover prices—what a great deal! I understand that accepting the 2 free books and gift places me under no obligation ever to buy any books. I can always return a shipment and cancel at any time. Even if I never buy another book from Harlequin, the 2 free books and gift are mine to keep forever.

106 HDN DNTZ
306 HDN DNT2

Name	(PLEASE PRINT)

Address	Apt.#

City	State/Prov.	Zip/Postal Code

* Terms and prices subject to change without notice. Sales tax applicable in N.Y.
** Canadian residents will be charged applicable provincial taxes and GST.
   All orders subject to approval. Offer limited to one per household and not valid to current Harlequin Presents® subscribers.
® are registered trademarks of Harlequin Enterprises Limited.

PRES02   ©2001 Harlequin Enterprises Limited

The world's bestselling romance series.

HARLEQUIN®
Presents~

Seduction and Passion Guaranteed!

GREEK TYCOONS

**They're the men who have everything—
except a bride...**

Wealth, power, charm—what else could a
heart-stoppingly handsome tycoon need? In the
GREEK TYCOONS miniseries you have already
been introduced to some gorgeous Greek
multimillionaires who are in need of wives.

Bestselling author *Jacqueline Baird* presents

THE GREEK TYCOON'S REVENGE
Harlequin Presents, #2266
Available in August

Marcus had found Eloise and he wants revenge—by
making Eloise his mistress for one year!

This tycoon has met his match, and he's decided he *has* to
have her...*whatever* that takes!

**Pick up a Harlequin Presents® novel and you will
enter a world of spine-tingling passion and
provocative, tantalizing romance!**

HARLEQUIN®
Makes any time special ®

*Available wherever
Harlequin books
are sold.*

HPGT07